She should have said something...

Eli's hands wove through Reagan's hair and kept her face turned up to his. "You never have to apologize for looking at me, Reagan. Ever."

"Things are different now, Eli. We both know it. If we can just get through—"

His hands tightened in her hair the second before his mouth crushed down on hers. Lips and teeth and tongue, all demanding and wanting and wet heat. She ached with need and hunger, ached in a way she'd forgotten she could feel.

Every thrust of his tongue demanded her response, refused to allow her to think, gave her no quarter except to touch him and move with him, to feel the hard muscle under his soft skin. She wanted everything he offered. Everything.

Reagan had missed this ravenous sexual ache; she'd hungered for this fire that branded her. It burned her from the inside out and turned her reservations to ash.

Eli freed one hand from her hair and, gripping her belt loop, yanked her closer.

And, God forgive her, she fell willingly into her first love's embrace...

Dear Reader,

It's with absolute pleasure I am able to introduce you to Harding County, New Mexico. It's a land of grassy plains that give themselves up to the beauty of the Sangre de Christo Mountains, a range that is in some places sparse and in others the most beautiful country you've ever seen.

When his father passes away, Elijah, the oldest of the three Covington boys, comes home after fourteen years away. He's reunited with the beautiful Reagan Matthews, the woman he loved and left behind—the only woman he's *ever* loved. And it's an emotional, passionate, thoroughly satisfying ride!

Having lived on a ranch myself in New Mexico after marrying my very own cowboy, I have to tell you that there are a few things in each of the Covington books that I've experienced firsthand, but I'm not telling which ones. Rest assured that every character and every situation is entirely a product of my imagination, though.

The one thing I *can* tell you with certainty? New Mexico's cowboys are every single bit as sexy as *anything* Texas has turned out.

Happy reading,

Kelli

Kelli Ireland

A Cowboy Returns

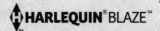

Recycling programs
for this product may
not exist in your area.

ISBN-13: 978-0-373-79862-9

A Cowboy Returns

Copyright © 2015 by Denise Tompkins

Printed in U.S.A.

www.Harlequin.com

Kelli Ireland spent a decade as a name on a door in corporate America. Unexpectedly liberated by Fate's sense of humor, she chose to carpe the diem and pursue her passion for writing. A fan of happily-ever-afters, she found she loved being the puppet master for the most unlikely couples. Seeing them through the best and worst of each other while helping them survive the joys and disasters of falling in love? Best. Thing. Ever. Visit Kelli's website at kelliireland.com.

Books by Kelli Ireland

HARLEQUIN BLAZE

Pleasure Before Business

Stripped Down
Wound Up
Pulled Under

To get the inside scoop on Harlequin Blaze and its talented writers, be sure to check out blazeauthors.com.

All backlist available in ebook format.

Visit the Author Profile page at Harlequin.com for more titles.

This book is for Vivian Arend,
one of the absolute best mentors a writer could
ever hope to find.

_1_

ELIJAH COVINGTON NEVER thought he'd find religion on a commuter flight, but when the tiny plane plummeted the last fifty feet to the runway, he prayed. Little more than a closed-cockpit crop duster, the little plane skipped down the cracked asphalt runway hard enough to compress his spine. He would have given anything for the firm's corporate jet and his chiropractor right about then.

Of course, he should probably just be grateful they weren't landing on a dirt strip. They'd had to circle several times while the neighboring rancher retrieved his cows from the runway. That had been bad enough.

The flight attendant made an inane joke at the pilot's expense, but Eli only half listened. Thumbing his smartphone on, he waited for a signal. His service indicator showed a single bar. _A single bar_.

"I'm in hell," he muttered, but that wasn't true. Hell undoubtedly had better cell service.

Scrolling through emails, he ignored the flight attendant's glare. He might have been obligated to come home to manage the distribution of his father's estate, but that didn't require he cut himself off from civilization entirely. With any luck, he could get to the ranch, go through the estate paperwork, file the will and be gone within the week. Had his old man been remotely organized, this could have been done by mail. And had the estate been reasonably solvent, they could have hired someone to manage the distributions altogether. No doubt, there wouldn't be any money.

That had to be why his youngest brother, Tyson, had emailed and asked him to come home and handle estate "issues." Otherwise? They never would have called him home. He'd have just received whatever his old man left him via certified mail.

Eli glanced out the window at the desert landscape. New Mexico always looked caught between centuries and droughts. The landscape was as foreign to him as Austin would be to his brothers. Here in Tucumcari, the wide plateau created a backdrop decorated with cedar shrubs, barbed wire fences and black grama grass. Cows outnumbered people twenty to one, and if you didn't drive a pickup, you'd better be riding a horse.

The only beef Eli cared about was braised, his vehicle was an Audi R8 and the only horses that mattered were under the hood.

He'd always been the piece that didn't fit this particular puzzle.

Elijah snorted and shook his head, pulling his small travel bag out from under his seat. *Might as well get this over with.*

Fifteen minutes later he was standing beside a tiny Ford Fiesta with a dented fender, an AM/FM radio and questionable air-conditioning. It was the better of the two cars available at the only car rental service in town.

"I'm in hell," he repeated, struggling against a temper he'd all but mastered over the past fourteen years.

Fourteen years.

He'd been gone almost as long as he'd lived here.

Peeling off his Canali suit jacket, he tossed it across the passenger seat before folding himself behind the wheel. A generous layer of grit on the rubber floor mat ground under his heel. The little car shimmied as the four-cylinder engine sputtered and choked before it caught and, obviously under duress, whined to life.

The rental attendant tipped the brim of his hat in salute and wandered inside the tiny office as Eli drove away. He hadn't remembered Elijah, or had pretended not to as a matter of convenience to avoid unnecessary chitchat. Small towns worked that way. You were either on the inside or exiled for life.

The next few days would be a lot of the same. Tight-knit communities were very unforgiving when one of their own escaped, and his leaving *had* been an escape. As well loved as his father had been, everyone saw his departure as a first-rate betrayal—oldest son to old man.

Elijah refused to feel guilty for wanting a different life, a *better* life. He had it now and hadn't asked for handouts along the way. He'd earned his place, and he wasn't sorry that place wasn't here. With one exception...

Caught up in his own thoughts, he ran one of the two traffic lights in town.

An extended-cab four-wheel-drive pickup swerved, brakes chattering and tires squealing. It hit the curb, skipping up and over with a hard bounce before coming to rest in the hedges in front of the Blue Swallow motel.

Heart lodged in his throat, Eli shut the little car down and left it in the middle of the road, racing toward the truck. He couldn't see anyone moving inside. Then a black-and-white head popped up and looked out the rear window.

A dog.

If anything, the dog seemed exhilarated at the wild ride, his feathery tail wagging with obvious enthusiasm.

Eli reached the driver's side and found a cowboy-hatted individual slumped forward, forehead against the steering wheel, arms lax, hands resting next to trim thighs. *A woman.* He reached for the truck door. The dog objected, going from excited to back-the-hell-off between breaths. The animal crossed his owner and bared his teeth in a feral growl, blatantly daring Eli to open the door.

Not interested in losing any body parts, Eli knocked on the window hard enough to rouse the woman.

She rolled her head to the side, green eyes narrowed in an impressive glare. The moment those eyes focused on Eli, they flared with almost-comedic alarm. Almost.

Because his did the same thing.

Reagan Armstrong.

The one person he'd intended to avoid altogether stared at him in utter disbelief. Her mouth hung open in shock. She didn't move.

History rose up between them, an invisible, insurmountable wall of differences that stole every word that might have allayed old hurts or bridged the gap of time to allow them to communicate. At least while he was here.

Leaning one arm against the truck's door frame, Eli gave a small jerk of his chin. "Reagan? Lower your window."

She mouthed something that, if it matched the look in her eyes, was seriously foul.

He was prepared for that. What he wasn't prepared

for was for her to shove the door open. The mirror folded as it nailed his shoulder. Then the hot metal of the door's edge slammed into his sternum hard enough he wasn't sure if he'd been burned or if the bone had cracked or both.

She spoke before her boots hit the dirt, her voice as smooth as the truck's diesel engine. "Well, well. If it isn't Elijah Covington. Or would that be Mr. Covington, Esquire, since you're an Austin attorney now? Just what you always wanted—bigger, better and worlds away from here—so I suppose congratulations would be appropriate. I mean, you made it out, made your way and managed to break your word, all in one impressive feat."

His brows drew together. "What are you talking about, 'break my word'?"

"You said you'd come home. Promised, in fact. But I'd be willing to bet you hit the county line at a dead run and never thought about us again. Good on you, Esquire." The last was offered with near indifference or would have been if she hadn't begun to clap slowly for emphasis.

It was that last action that betrayed her, because, despite their fourteen years apart, Eli knew her.

The aged and seasoned hurt that lurked beneath the surface of her words sliced through his conscience with cold efficiency. He'd wanted her to come with him, but she'd made it clear her life was here. And his life could never be here.

"You knew we wanted different things. I was never going to fit in here. Not like you did. My dad. My brothers. Leaving was my only option. And I didn't just skip out on you." Running his hands through his hair, he huffed out a heavy breath. "Look, Reagan," he started, and then the wind shifted, carrying her smell to him, all fresh-cut hay and sunshine on warm skin.

Overwhelmed with sensory memories, his gaze homed in on lips that parted in almost curious shock. And just like that, she was the girl he'd loved. And yet, with time and distance, she had somehow evolved into more.

She'd always been his sun, chasing away the shadows he hadn't been able to banish himself. Unwelcome memories of yesteryear hovered at the fringes of his consciousness. He needed to touch her, needed the tenderness he'd always found waiting in her.

He closed the distance between them. His lips closed over hers and he pulled her into his embrace. The shock of cinnamon on his tongue told him she still loved Big Red gum, and the flavor transferred between them. Her lips were soft, pliable and so familiar his heart ached with the memories of a thousand and more shared moments. Being here, in New Mexico, didn't hurt so much with her in his arms.

He wasn't only "Covington's oldest boy." He wasn't burdened with the unshakable disappointment his father had found in him. He wasn't a failure of an older brother. He was Eli. Just Eli. And he could survive that.

His troubles became manageable as their tongues touched, tentative for the briefest moment. Then he took over the kiss. Dominating the moment, he took comfort in her nearness and yelped like a scolded pup when she bit his lip. Hard.

Parking both hands on his chest, she shoved and shouted, "What in the Sam Hill are you doing?" Eyes wild, she dragged a hand over her mouth. "You don't waltz into town after fourteen years, run me off the

road and then… You don't… You can't kiss me like…
like…you *ass*!"

"'Ass'? I kiss you and you call me an *ass*?" Eli's lips
thinned as his once-infamous temper, second only to
hers and all but squashed under years of educational and
professional training, raced forward like a laser-guided
missile, target locked, impact imminent. "I'm going to
point out the obvious here, Reagan. You kissed me, too."

"I didn't… That is… No. There was no mutual…
No, I didn't!" Chest heaving, she drove a finger into his
chest. "Why are you even here? The funeral was two
freaking weeks ago. You should've been here *then*. But
you show up now, expecting everyone to bend to your
expectations. That's so typical, Eli. It's always been the
way you operate," she snapped, backing up until she
bumped into her truck. She hopped in, never taking her
eyes off him. "You haven't changed at all. You're still
smart as shit when it comes to business and dumb as
dirt when it comes to people."

"Hey," he objected, but she powered on without
pause.

"You're too late to do any good, Eli, but, then, you
taught me what to expect a long time ago. I'd truly
thought you'd show for the funeral, though. For your
blood." She looked him up and down with a critical eye
as she delivered the blow he should've anticipated but
never saw coming. "I might have been your girlfriend
once, but Cade and Tyson are your brothers, Eli. They
needed you." Her gaze met his, anger turning the normally moss green color of her eyes deep and vibrant.
"They needed you here to help them manage the mess
your old man left behind, but you clearly couldn't put
your high-society life aside for a few days to come home

and help them out of the bind they're in. You never could be bothered. Not for them. Not for anyone."

She moved to slam the door, but he grabbed it, stepping close. "That's why I'm here now—to probate my father's estate. But that's irrelevant. You don't get to sit there in your shiny truck, that captain's chair your personal throne, and pass judgment on me, Armstrong."

Jerking away as if struck, she stared at him with wide eyes. "It hasn't been 'Armstrong' for eight years. It's Matthews. And to you? *Dr.* Matthews. Nothing less, and never, ever anything more. Now let go of the door, Eli."

His hand fell away from the truck.

She'd married Luke Matthews. He'd had no idea.

The reality he'd likely see her and Luke together while in town made Eli's stomach lurch up his throat until he seriously wondered if he might puke. Wouldn't that be awesome.

Then there was the fact she was a doctor. From the size of her truck and the type of work boxes, he didn't have to ask what kind. A vet. She'd always wanted to be a large-animal vet.

He cleared his throat once, then twice, before he managed to croak, "Great. Happy for you."

Slamming the truck door shut, she made it a point to click the locks down. Couldn't get much clearer than that.

Her dog whined loud enough for Eli to hear the cry over the soft rumble of the truck's engine. Reagan absently soothed the animal, her hand shaking.

Eli could totally relate. Years in court had trained him to present a totally calm and controlled exterior under extreme pressure. That didn't mean his insides weren't rattling, though. The emotions buffering him now were both uncomfortable and unrecognizable. But there was no point examining them too closely. This visit didn't center around assuaging years of curiosity and doubt; nor did it have anything to do with healing old hurts. It was about finally closing this part of his life. Permanently.

Swallowing his anger and determined to keep things civil, he motioned for her to roll her window down.

Green eyes that had always before met his with open trust and absolute passion narrowed and glared. She punctuated the stare with a one-fingered salute. Without waiting for him to move, she slammed the truck into Reverse and punched the accelerator.

He leaped aside with a shouted curse.

The truck surged off the curb, suspension squeaking in protest. She shifted the truck into gear and, leaning on the accelerator, she rapidly put distance between them.

The dog, its tail still wagging, watched him with open curiosity thought the rear window.

Closing his eyes, Eli parked his fists on his hips and let his chin fall to his chest.

What the hell am I doing here?

"Settling an old debt," he answered quietly. He was here to make sure his brothers were okay. Yet according to Reagan, he was already too late for that.

Trying to wipe the unforgettable taste of her off his lips, he crossed the still-vacant street and crammed himself into the compact car before making a left and heading up Highway 54.

He was going to get this done and get gone. That would spare everyone involved any further awkwardness. Then he'd return to Austin, to the career he excelled at and the life he'd carved out for himself.

And Reagan was right. He wouldn't look back.

REAGAN MATTHEWS MUSCLED her heavy-duty truck around the corner and shot down the highway as hard and fast as the GMC would go. She had to put distance between herself and that…that…*man*.

But it wasn't just the man—it was the memories. She'd tried to put up a good front with Eli, to come across as both indifferent and controlled. Even *she* knew she'd botched it up and let emotion get the best of her. The apathy she'd dug for had been, at best, a shaky mirage. A strong gust of wind would have swept the bulk of it away, a million seeds of discontent that simply wanted answers.

But then he'd kissed her.

If her apathy hadn't stood a chance against a simple breeze, it couldn't hold out hope for survival when faced with the force of nature that *was* Elijah Covington.

He'd been the sole shareholder of her heart, the one thing she was sure she couldn't live without. All those days spent at the river, just the two of them listening to music, talking, watching the sunset against the Sangre de Cristo Mountains. Then there were the nights. Hours spent stargazing and more hours spent discovering each other, learning the touches that elicited the most pleasure, the sensitive spots to kiss softly, the right time to love gently and the time to let it all go and be as wild and free as the world around them.

Then he'd left.

So many years she'd held out hope he'd come back. She'd been the talk of the town for so long, first with shared hope, then pity and then the fool who simply couldn't let go of a man long gone. She'd never stopped loving him. She'd just stopped looking for him.

Reagan traced her numb lips with trembling fingers. Her chest had constricted to the point she couldn't draw even half a breath. But her heart… She rubbed her sternum. Her heart hadn't hurt this bad in years, and wasn't that a testament to the way she'd lived her life.

She allowed reality to sink in, accepting that Eli'd had his arms around her again, and it had felt as familiar as it did foreign. A broken sob ripped out of her chest. She'd spent the past fourteen years trying not to drown in heartache and regrets. Then he showed up and, with a single kiss, pulled her under those dark emotional waters again. He acted as if it had meant as little to him as if he were ordering a cup of coffee to go.

When she'd broken away, she'd begun to sink.

Taking the first dirt road she came to, she slid to a stop, dust billowing around her. She rested her head on the steering wheel and rolled her forehead back and forth, trying to force her roiling thoughts to fall into place.

She'd have to repair the Blue Swallow's landscaping. But the damage *really* hadn't been her fault. Most people reacted poorly when a ghost ran them off the road.

Elijah Covington.

"Not a ghost," she said, voice hoarse. "Just a memory. A…mistake."

But that wasn't true, either. Loving him had never been a mistake. Holding on to the faith he'd figure out he belonged here, too? That she was the one for him? Those were her major screwups, the two things that had given him the power to thoroughly and effectively decimate her heart.

Swiping her cowboy hat off, she cursed as she rewound her hair and tucked it under the hat. "It's been fourteen years now, Matthews. You've moved on. You have a career and a life story, neither of which include him."

She didn't have much of a life at the moment, though. What she had were long, backbreaking days and endless, lonely nights.

In the passenger seat, her dog, Brisket, whined.

"It's fine. I'm fine." Untucking her shirt, she wiped the sweat—*not* tears—off her face.

The iPad alarm sounded. She glanced at the screen with a physical wince. Almost nine. She was due at the Jensen place in a little less than an hour to draw up health papers on their steers before they shipped the yearlings to the livestock auction in nearby Dalhart, Texas.

Scrubbing her hands over her face, she forced a deep breath. All right. Eli had come home. So what? He was fast-flowing water under the charred remnants of a bridge burned long ago. She could avoid him for however long he was here. And knowing him, it would only be temporary. He had run before; he would run again. That was what he was good at, after all.

Shifting the truck into Reverse, she backed out onto the highway as a faded red car started up the two-lane highway from the boulevard. Slow but sure, the car closed in on her. The driver was hunched over the wheel as if he were nothing but an origami miniature of a large man. Dark hair blew in the breeze from the open window. Large hands wrung the steering wheel. If the poor thing had been alive, he'd have killed it a thousand times over.

Eli.

Reagan punched the accelerator. Her tires chirped on the hot asphalt before gaining hold. The truck belched and then roared to life. She watched in the rearview mirror as the little red car disappeared in a dense cloud of diesel exhaust.

The truck's tires slipped off the highway shoulder and into soft sand, forcing her attention to the road. Overcorrecting, she crossed into the opposite lane before muscling the truck onto her side of the road again.

Heat burned up her neck and settled on her cheeks. *Freaking wonderful, Matthews. Exactly the kind of impression you wanted to leave him with.* Then she grinned. She'd just filled the guy's car with a solid layer of diesel exhaust. Sure, she'd almost wrecked her truck.

It was totally worth it.

2

THREE HOURS LATER, Reagan wiped the sweat from her brow with a grungy bandana. "Is it me or is it about a hundred and ten out here today?"

"Only supposed to be about ninety." Tyson Covington, youngest of the three Covington brothers, tipped the brim of his hat up and leaned on the saddle horn to grin down at her. "I'm no expert in female anatomy, but I'd say you're far too young for hot flashes, Doc."

She barked out a laugh. "Not an expert in female anatomy, huh? The only person in Harding County who's seen more action than you, Ty, is the gynecologist, and that's only because he's been in practice longer than you've been alive."

Ty's grin widened. "I suppose I'll just have to work harder to catch up then, won't I?"

Her snort was answer enough. Turning back to the chute, she called out, "Push 'em through, gentlemen."

"You heard Doc Matthews," Ty shouted to the other cowboys. "Let's get the first truck backed up and help the Jensens make a little money." He let out a sharp whistle as he wheeled his horse around and pushed his way into the thick of things.

She grabbed her pad and jotted down a couple of notes as the semi parked, trailer gate open to the chute. The herd looked pretty good. A few were underweight, but calves sometimes lost a little mass to stress when they were gathered and penned. They'd also lose a bit of water weight when they shipped, but it would be easy to replace that. Picking up her vaccine gun, she climbed up the pipe panel and started inoculating the animals as they moved by.

Once the first group of animals were loaded, they began sorting the second pen. Bawling protests decorated the dusty air. Cowboys called to each other as they moved the calves and pushed the current bunch down the chute, peeling off those Reagan indicated she wanted to assess a little closer. One truck driver after another climbed around shipping trailers like monkeys, opening and closing interior gates to make sure the weight distribution of the oncoming cattle was beneficial for the haul to the sale ring.

A larger yearling turned back. Nose high, the whites of his eyes showed as he tried to work his way against the flow.

Reagan scanned the corral. "Brisket!"

A blue merle body darted between the men and their horses, arrowing toward her. The Border collie stopped twenty feet away, crouched and ready, focused on her as he waited for instruction. With a short whistle and pointed finger toward the offender, she set him loose.

The dog wove through the masses. Reaching the bottleneck, he started nipping with a strike-retreat-strike approach, turning the steer around and driving the herd forward with unparalleled efficiency.

It took a couple more hours to sort the remaining calves, and Reagan was officially exhausted by the time they finished. Carol Jensen approached her with a tall glass of tea, a barbecue sandwich wrapped in waxed paper, and a genuine smile. Such a nice person, and her husband was much the same.

Accepting the drink first, Reagan sighed. "Thanks, Carol."

"What was the total count?"

"We vaccinated and loaded 812 today. I held back a handful that weren't ready or seemed a little sickly to ship to market. The other cows are ready to be driven to the bull pasture for breeding. Overall, with price-per-pound holding steady at $212 a hundredweight? Should be a very profitable day."

"Glad to hear it." Reaching into her pocket, Carol pulled out a second sandwich. "Brisket around?"

Reagan smiled and shook her head as the dog trotted up and sat at the other woman's feet. "No wonder he likes to visit you."

"He works hard enough he should probably be paid day wages."

"We talked about it, but he decided long ago that self-employment taxes suck. Besides, I'm pretty sure he prefers to be paid with barbecue."

In apparent agreement, Brisket took his sandwich and sprinted across the arena. He dropped down in the shade of the barn and began ripping off the waxed paper to get to the treat, his tail thumping a happy beat.

Ty sauntered over, his horse's reins draped loosely over his shoulder. The giant quarter horse followed along, appearing to be more docile pet than high-dollar cutting horse. Ty smiled and winked, the picture of innocence. "You have another sandwich for a starving man, Mrs. Jensen?"

"You're a menace to the female population," Carol

said primly. Still, she started to head for the house. "I'll bring you a couple sandwiches. You want tea or lemonade?"

"Whatever you have is fine. I'd get it myself, but I'm too dirty to do much more than strip down and wash in the stock tank."

Reagan hid her grin when Carol blushed.

Flustered, the woman fled.

"You're a nuisance, Ty." Reagan finished her sandwich and leaned against the corral fence, one boot heel hung on a rail.

"I'm harmless," he countered, pulling his hat off and shaking out light brown hair darkened with sweat.

"You're as harmless as a bad case of ringworm. Treatable, but still a pain in the ass."

Denim-blue eyes sparkled with mischief. "Treatable, am I? Come over tonight and I'll play patient to your doctor."

Reagan pulled her vaccine gun out, the massive needle glinting in the bright sunlight. "Why wait? Drop your drawers, and I'll take care of you right this minute."

Ty blanched. "Not exactly the kind of action I had in mind if my pants came off."

One corner of her mouth curled up. "Chicken shit."

"Hey, if you weren't so hot, I wouldn't feel compelled to flirt."

This time she laughed. "Ty, you'd flirt with an octogenarian if she was the only woman around. You can't help yourself."

His horse nosed him, shoving him toward her a step. "You know it's all in fun."

She waggled the vaccine gun at him and fought the urge to smile. "Only because my gun's bigger."

"That's an unfair comparison. You've never seen my gun."

"No offense, but I'm not interested in your caliber." Her stomach tightened at the memory of just what caliber she had once been *very* interested in—the same caliber that forced her off the road only hours earlier. Keeping busy had helped her forget him, but now her mind raced.

Chewing her bottom lip, she glanced at Ty. "Today, in town, I…well, I was run off the road by…"

He scrutinized her, and Reagan wondered what he saw. When he sobered, she knew. The barbecue sandwich that had cut through hunger pangs only moments ago now sat like a lead cannonball in her stomach. She swallowed convulsively. It took a minute to work the question around the emotion lodged in her throat. "What's he doing here, Ty?"

Dark brows winged down and he shoved sunglasses on to cover his eyes. "I asked Eli to come home for this thing involving Dad."

Her chin snapped around. "Doesn't the fact you had to *ask* him to come home tell you where he stands in all of this?"

"He should be here, Reagan. It's his mess and his legacy as much as it is ours." Full lips thinned. "Cade and I are going to need his help to sort out the mess Dad left us in. Our best chance at saving the ranch involves Eli…and you."

The blood drained from her face at being paired, even loosely, in a sentence with Eli. "You can't be sure your herd's got Shipping Fever until the lab results come back and I get out there and look at the steer we drew from."

"I grew up around this stuff. I know what it is." He

snorted and shook his head, hooking one arm through the pipe panel. "It's going to ruin Dad's perfect reputation."

"He wasn't perfect," she said softly, remembering how Mr. Covington had always been so cold and rigid in his expectations of Eli. Those expectations had succeeded in driving Eli away for good, and she'd never forgive the old man for it.

Carol's return with two sandwiches and a giant glass of lemonade interrupted the conversation. She'd also brought Ty cookies. "I thought you might want something sweet."

Reagan fought the urge to steal a cookie.

As if the conversation hadn't been deadly serious only moments before, Ty looked at the older woman and grinned wide enough to reveal a single dimple. "You're an angel, Mrs. Jensen. You ever get tired of Mr. Jensen, you pack up and we'll run away together."

She flushed prettily. "You're incorrigible, Ty."

"Can't blame a man for being attracted to a pretty woman…Carol."

Reagan only half listened as Ty bantered with Carol and then a few of the day workers as he ate his sandwiches. She offered absent, one-word answers when someone said something directly to her, but she couldn't manage to tease and joke in return.

"Hey."

She glanced up to find her and Ty alone again. Coughing, she nodded. "Yeah."

Ty ran a hand around the nape of his neck. "I probably should have warned you Eli was coming home."

She winced at his name.

"I just wasn't sure how to bring it up."

She waved a hand in dismissal, but the words that

matched the gesture wouldn't come. Her chest was too tight. Shrouded in panic, she pushed off the fence. It had been years since this had happened, since she'd given in to the devastating loss that had changed the course of her life and affected every aspect of it, from what she'd taken in school to five years of marriage.

A hard gasp escaped her at the same time large hands spun her around. She said the only thing she could say to him. "Keep him away from me, Ty."

"You want the Bar C to use Doc Hollinsworth? I don't want to, but if you ask, I'll do it."

She swallowed convulsively. He was offering her a shameless out. All she had to do was seize it.

"You know we're in trouble," he continued. "None of us are sure just how bad it's going to get, but I'll wager my assless chaps it's going to get ugly. We've got to have a vet on call. You know that, too. I can't imagine Eli's going to keep his share of the cows, even if they survive. Probably ship them off as soon as we can prove they aren't infected. If that's the case, I can try to put off getting the shipping papers until after Eli's gone, maybe handle that part myself—me or Cade, anyway—and just send Eli the check."

She straightened. "Call me when you're ready. Hollinsworth isn't half the man I am."

Ty grinned, but it didn't lessen the tight lines at the corners of his eyes or the crease between his brows. "Hell, Reagan, not many of us are." Curling a finger under her chin, he nudged her face up. "You've managed really well."

Her laugh was bitter. "Survival isn't admirable, Ty. It's the only option they ever left me with, him and Luke."

"Luke didn't die on you on purpose."

She nodded, swiping viciously at the tears that fell

for the loss of each man. "He might not have done it on purpose, but gone is gone. The only difference between Luke and Eli?" Backing away from Ty, she didn't bother to try to hide her misery. "Luke didn't have a choice. Eli did. But in the end? They both left me."

Spinning on her heel, she called hoarsely for Brisket. The dog leaped into the truck bed, and she didn't try to coax him into the cab.

Vaulting herself into the seat behind the wheel, she cranked the engine and took off, pretending not to hear Ty calling her name.

There was nothing left to say.

3

ELI MADE THE 120-mile drive to the Clayton County courthouse in average time considering his rental car was powered by little more than a two-stroke lawn-mower engine.

His first order of business was to determine whether or not anything had been filed on his old man's behalf or—worse—against the estate. Nothing showed up, so he went through the rest of the probate process.

Privately, he was grateful for the mundane tasks. They kept his mind busy, kept him from thinking too much. He made the appropriate inquiries at the court-house and filed the required documents as the estate's representative. Then he'd gone to the newspaper to ar-range for the mandatory ads to run in the classifieds. That done, he started for the ranch.

Less than ten miles from the courthouse, he was the only car on the highway. No surprise. The locals would consider traffic heavy if they passed a dozen cars. He was as far from Austin's bumper-to-bumper lifestyle as he could get. Considering the clown car and his sur-real surroundings, it was as if he'd been fired from civ-ilization's cannon into the wilds of wide-open space.

Every instinct he had screamed the landing was going to suck. Bad.

The memory of Reagan—her summertime smell, her cinnamon taste, her feminine strength, her lean body—had haunted him all morning.

She'd always been at the heart of the community. It made sense, then, that she'd married the community's son.

Everyone loved Luke. He was the kind who stopped to help a stranded motorist and not only fixed their car but topped off their gas and gave them food and a fresh set of directions before sending them on their way. Always neighborly, he'd be the first to volunteer for day work during shipping season. He'd be the last to leave. As a kid, every son had been compared to Luke—his dad had told him several times he would have preferred Luke as a son over him any day. Even Reagan's mother had expressed her opinion, pushing her daughter toward Saint Luke—and away from Eli. She must have been overjoyed when Reagan married the right man.

Eli would put money on it the guy had evolved to the ultimate cowboy, the type of man every boy wanted to grow up to be. He and Eli had always been casual friends, but at the moment? Eli hated every damn cell in the man's body.

Rolling the car window down, he breathed in the dry air. New Mexico's unpopulated roads and wide-open spaces never failed to press their beauty on him without apology—right before they reminded him how insignificant he was.

He'd never been able to accomplish enough to stand out as his own man, always living in his father's shadow. Never Elijah Covington, but always Max Covington's boy. And even in that, the only thing that set him apart was that he was the eldest of the three. His greatest distinction was that he'd been his dad's biggest disappointment. Never quite country enough, never quite smart enough, never quite proud enough of his name, just… never quite enough.

The only one who'd ever made him feel he was more, could *be* more, had been Reagan.

Seeing her today had shaken him. Hard. She'd been more beautiful than he remembered, those moss green eyes set in a deceptively feminine face. Most people just saw a pretty girl who'd make a good rancher's wife. He'd always known there was far more to her than that. It had terrified him they'd both end up doing exactly what the community expected of them—him taking over his father's ranching operation, and her staying on in the little town because she loved her man.

She *had* stayed, but not for reasons he'd ever understood.

Emotions whipped through him as unchecked as spring winds, tearing up certain pieces of his life and battering others until he was a mess of overlapping memories. When he finally reached the right road, Eli pointed the little car across the first of eleven cattle guard and started through the sand hills. It was a different world out here, yet nothing had changed. He could find his way through this alien landscape with his eyes closed.

Rounding a corner, he rolled to a stop. Cows blocked the road, completely unconcerned with either him or his cartoon car. Waving his arm out the window and shouting, pair after pair of huge brown eyes lifted to blink at him. He honked and snorted at the almost comical beep that made him think of circus cars that dumped out twenty clowns in the ring.

"I am *not* getting out of this car," he shouted at them. Laying on the horn, he whistled and eased into the mass of bodies. Slowly, the herd began to move off.

Eli tunneled his fingers through his hair and fought the urge to turn the car around. He could get to Amarillo and catch a flight back to Austin tonight, be in his own bed by midnight and back in the office first thing tomorrow morning. And if it weren't for the fact Tyson had asked for help, he would have done just that.

Damn it.

His youngest brother had never asked him for anything. Ever. The realization yoked him with heavy guilt. He'd do this for Ty and leave.

And what about Cade? his conscience whispered.

Oh, Cade had asked him for something once, had asked for the one thing he couldn't give. He'd never forgiven Eli for saying no, either.

Eli whispered dire threats to the little car as it struggled up the final hill. It peaked and the world opened up. From the Sangre de Cristo mountain range to the west, the uninterrupted northern horizon and the plains to the east, open range spread before him with regal silence. His breath caught and his chest ached.

This would always be his place, his heritage and his home. But it seemed as foreign to him as another country, as if a passport should be required to visit his past. He was nothing more than a visitor and an unwelcome one, at that. Trying to ignore the undeniable beauty of the land and the way it called to him, soft and familiar, he put the car in gear, starting forward again. The car rattled over the washboard road. A bolt fell out from under the dash and clunked against the passenger floorboard as Eli's teeth clattered together.

A dust trail caught his eye. Somebody was tearing

through the sand hills. If Eli'd had a four-wheel drive, he would've ducked down a side road to avoid being seen. In this thing? He'd be dooming himself to walking, and it was way too far to the ranch to run the risk. Instead, he eased forward at the same time he rolled his window up. It would be easy enough to stay focused on the road and ignore whoever passed him. Might be the smartest thing to do, too.

He gained momentum heading down the hill, the little car bucking over the rutted road. A pickup truck roared by. Eli didn't look up. Instead, he leaned on the accelerator, jaw tight, wheel strangled in a death grip. Habit had him flipping a hand up in absent greeting. Brake lights lit up the rearview mirror as the truck fishtailed to a stop.

Curiosity got the better of Eli. He slowed as he watched the driver's side door swing open. The driver jumped down, boots stirring up small puffs of dust as he stormed toward the slowing car. Tall and clearly furious, the man yanked his hat off and tossed it aside without a care. Long legs ate up the distance between them. Lips thinned and eyes hardened the closer the guy came.

Eli let the car drift to a stop even as his stomach went into free fall. His mouth was so dry he couldn't have share-cropped the space without subsidized water rights. Slipping the car into Park, he couldn't make himself stop staring until the man was so close Eli could only see his torso in the little mirror.

Eli reached for the door handle.

The man beat him to it, yanking the door open. "Get out."

Eli's jaw set. "Out of the car or out of town?"

"Car first, town second." The low voice was so raw it sounded like it had been dragged over sharp gravel.

His hands ached with the urge to clench into tight fists. "That's not your call."

Work-roughened hands reached into the car.

Shoving the man away, Eli lunged to stand. "What's your—" A meaty fist connected with his jaw, whipping his head to the side. Stars exploded in his vision. Shaking his head, he rounded on the man, considering him through narrowed eyes. "What the he—" A short jab split his lip. "That's. It."

Eli threw himself into the fight. Grunting as the other man's fist connected with his ribs, he spun and kicked out. He connected with a hip, forcing the bastard off him.

The man regained his balance and, chest heaving, charged Eli.

They went down in a heap, arms swinging and legs kicking as they pummeled each other for all they were worth. A hard shot to Eli's temple made him see double. The guy grabbed him by the front of his oxford and twisted so he knelt over Eli, fist raised.

Eli set his jaw. He wouldn't fight anymore. Not like this.

"You sorry son of a bitch," the man gasped. "All these years. You been gone all these years. Why now?"

Eli swallowed hard. "It's good to see you, too, brother."

Cade Covington shoved off Eli, panting. "Can't say the same."

Seemed karma was determined to put the screws to him by dumping every ounce of history in his lap all at once.

Excellent.

Eli dabbed his split lip with his shirttail. "You still hit like a freaking truck."

"You used to be faster." Cade shook out his fist. "What're you doing here, Eli?"

Cade's tone was cold and Eli glanced at his brother. "Ty didn't tell you?"

"Tell me what?" Cade asked, the words flat.

"He asked me to come home and probate the estate."

His brother cursed, low and harsh.

"I'll take that as a no." Eli leaned against the little clown car and, one at a time, emptied his shoes of sand.

Cade turned away, his voice carrying on the wind. "I've got this covered. We don't need your brand of help."

The words hit Eli harder than any of Cade's blows. He watched his younger brother, the middle of the three of them, retrieve his hat and head for his truck, his gait as long and sure as ever.

"I'll see this through," Eli called after him.

Cade shook his head, slapping his hat against his thigh as he paused beside his idling truck. "Why bother? You don't want to be here, and we don't want you. So just…go on. Get back to Austin and do whatever it is you do down there."

Eli clenched his jaw so tight his molars ached. His nostrils flared on each exhale. "I have a client roster that proves I finish what I start."

Cade settled his hat on his head and glanced over his shoulder. "A client roster, huh?" He shook his head and grinned sardonically. "And how many of those clients have you stuck by through the years, Eli? How many have you seen through the hard times because it was the right thing to do?" When Eli didn't answer, Cade shook his head, grin fading. "They *pay you* to stick. You don't do it because it's the right thing, and that makes all the difference."

"I've never walked out on my professional responsibilities," Eli snapped.

"Then I can honestly say I wish we'd been professional associates instead of brothers." Slamming the driver's door behind him, Cade shifted the truck into Drive and took off.

Hurt and anger warred for dominance, an internal battle that bloodied Eli with every volley. *Who the hell does Cade think he is?*

The idea that he could leave this whole mess to someone else crossed his mind again. He could send a check to cover the attorney's fees, let it be someone else's headache. Epic temptation that it was, it would only reinforce Cade's opinion that he didn't care about his family.

Eli glared down the empty dirt road. He might be a lot of things, but a quitter? No. His leaving had been about survival and what was best for everyone. If Cade didn't get that?

"Screw him." Folding himself gingerly into the car, he winced as it gained speed and resumed rattling over the dirt road. Each jarring bump hammered every new bruise. By the time Eli reached Highway 102, he was pretty sure at least two fillings were loose.

He had no idea how he would manage staying at the ranch with Cade and Ty, but there wasn't a decent hotel within a hundred miles. What there was would be historic—thereby archaic—and that translated to dial-up internet if he was lucky, rotary phones and curious proprietors. The ranch would at least have a rudimentary office. His brothers might not appreciate his presence, but one-third of the house was his, and he intended to put it to use before deeding it to them jointly. Breaking all ties with this place was long past due.

Eli buzzed by the ranch's main gate. The black iron arch over the gate had the ranch's name centered at the top arch, the family name below. Their individual brands were showcased on either side of the ranch name. His, the E-bar C, was to the right.

The battered mailbox stood weather-beaten and worn as ever. The red flag hung broken and listless, the ever-present breeze swinging it back and forth sporadically. Behind the mailbox stood the metal road sign—Road to Perdition.

He'd helped weld and post it with his old man's help. He'd been…what? Eleven? Twelve? The irony had been lost on him at the time. Now? Now it just seemed prophetic. His mother had died two years later and cemented his understanding of perdition. Spiritual ruin. Utter destruction. Hell.

He passed under the sign and onto Covington land.

Tension built in knots across his shoulders, spreading down each side of his spine the farther down the road he went. Long-suppressed memories were close enough to the surface to shove into his consciousness. They dragged him through an entire lifetime of highs and lows that he'd lived in the measly nineteen years he'd been here. So much to remember. So much he wanted to forget. Too much to survive all over again. Shutting his thoughts out, he took in the landscape.

The range looked good. The pastures had benefited from heavier-than-usual summer rains, the black grama grass already heading out. To the west, the mountains rose in a wild spray of desert colors. Fences were tight. Windmills spun in lazy circles, pumping water in a slow but predictable push-pause, push-pause cadence. Yet for all that, something was wrong. It took him a minute to figure it out, but when he did, he felt like an idiot.

As pretty as everything appeared, the pastures were empty.

The ground around the stock tanks should have been soupy from cows stomping through the overflow. Not so.

Grass shouldn't be thickening along livestock trails. It was.

The roads shouldn't have been clear of cow pies and other evidence of a herd. They were.

This wasn't the picture of a working ranch but rather an idyllic snapshot of grasslands. Postcard perfect.

His brows drew together. It was the end of the stocker/grower season. His brothers should be getting ready to ship the contracted stocker steers to the feed yards, yet there was no evidence of activity. Anywhere. Following the road toward the main house, his confusion increased when he found the fields closest to the place empty. That should've been where his brothers were holding the cattle and where the work was happening.

Trying to sort out what might have gone wrong, he suddenly recalled Ty's email. His little brother had asked him to handle the estate's "issues." Eli had assumed his brother meant the difficulty of probating such a physically large estate without a will or, at the very least, without a sufficient will.

Then there was Reagan. She'd accused him of not being here to help his brothers.

Looking around as he pulled up to the main house, the inactivity made his skin tighten. The "issues" his youngest brother had mentioned were clearly going to be larger, *much* larger, than Eli had assumed.

He parked in the main house's half-circle drive. His childhood home hadn't changed at all, from the silver tin roof to the stone walls to the aged, wavy glass of the picture windows. The sense of familiarity sans family left him empty. Steeling himself, he stepped out of the car.

The first thing to strike him was the smell. Someone had cut hay, and recently. The rich, clean smell tickled his nose. Below that hovered the subtle, distinct aroma of ammonia that was inherent to large animals. The barn door squeaked as the breeze curled around the corner of the building to shove the door to and fro. And the sky—man, the sky was so much bigger and bluer than he remembered.

All of that he could break down and compartmentalize by sense. It was the massive quiet that demanded recognition, though, calling forward all those memories he'd been fighting to suppress. They echoed endlessly through the aching hollow of his chest.

Pocketing his keys, he dropped his bag and headed for the barn.

Somewhere nearby, a mule brayed.

Eli grinned. Before he'd left, Ty had been bottle-feeding a little jack. The thing had followed the kid around like a damn dog.

Not a kid anymore. Ty would have grown up while Eli was away. He wondered if Ty was half as big as his feet and awkwardness had forecast he'd be. A dull burn settled in his belly when he realized he might not recognize his little brother after so long.

Rubbing his abs, Eli slipped into the dim barn.

The smells of leather and horse sweat joined the mix, dragging his past forward. He'd lived out here as a kid. It had been the one place he'd been entirely comfortable, with the cowhands and the horses. Leaning into the tack room, he was surprised to see a few extra saddles. The ranch must've taken on more hands, but for what? With the empty fields, he couldn't imagine there would be enough work to justify the number of saddles on pegs or money to pay them.

Several horses stuck their heads over their stall doors and peered at him, curious.

He ran a hand around the base of his skull and pulled. A cloak of unease settled around him. It had to be coming here, to the ranch. *Back home.*

A diesel engine rumbled into the yard and saved him from that particular train of thought. Avoiding that sentimental bullshit was beyond necessary. As it was, his life was far too close to turning into a country song full of loss and longing. Eli didn't have room for those emotions.

And with Reagan married, he'd never chance that road again.

4

REAGAN PULLED UP in front of the southern corrals at the Covington place. Several trucks were parked at the bunkhouses, but she didn't see Ty's or Cade's anywhere. She had expected she'd beat Ty to the Bar C, but she'd thought Cade would be around. As serious as things were likely to get, she couldn't imagine the brothers would be too far out of pocket.

Grabbing the backpack she carried her paperwork and iPad in, she slid out of the truck. Brisket leaped down and trotted along beside her, eyes glued to her hands, as she strode toward the main bunkhouse. Chances were someone there would know where Cade had run off to.

"Can I help you?"

She stumbled to a stop. Numb, her hands hung at her sides. Her feet wouldn't move no matter what she silently shouted at them.

"I asked if I could help you."

She might have shaken her head. Could have been she was just shaking. She had no idea.

"Hey. I'm talking to you."

That dark chocolate voice wound around her chest

and tightened, and her heart suddenly didn't have enough room to hammer so wildly. She wondered if it would break free of her ribs or just break. *Are there even enough pieces left?*

Brisket pressed up against her legs as he looked over his shoulder.

"That dog… Reagan?"

Steeling herself, hands fisting, she turned with incrementally small steps. "Yeah?"

"Why didn't you answer me?" he asked, exasperation woven through the question.

She shrugged as she mentally reached for her pride. "I figured I'd weigh the odds of you assaulting me again if I turned around. But with Brisket out of the truck this time, I'm feeling lucky."

He smiled slowly. "Feeling lucky, huh? I didn't think married women were supposed to cop to that with another man."

Ice lodged in her chest and her vision wavered through unexpected tears even as a fierce blush stole up her neck and across her cheeks. "Go to hell, Esquire. It's right back the way you came, so you shouldn't have trouble finding your way."

The smile faded. "Look, I'm sorry. I shouldn't have kissed you earlier."

His apology caught her off guard. Picking up her pack, she called Brisket to her as she started toward the bunkhouse again. "Stick with the insults. They go with the suit better than apologies."

"I didn't know you were married." His irritation escalated with every word. "And stop calling me Esquire."

She didn't really want to be petty, fought not to smile. And lost. Pausing, she glanced over her shoulder. The smile morphed from snarky to humorless when their eyes met. "But it fits you so well. There's the attorney thing, but there's also the fact you're out here—" she looked him over just as she had earlier, head to toe "—apparently rolling around in cow shit while wearing designer duds I bet were featured in your namesake's magazine. Esquire, it is."

"I don't remember you being so bitter," he said, absently brushing at his clothes.

"And I don't remember you being so worried about how you looked or what people thought," she volleyed.

Something wounded passed through his gaze. "Then you weren't paying attention."

The breeze shifted. Eli's cologne carried across the air, teasing her with its rich, crisp scent. She drew a breath, intent on offering him a creative suggestion on what to do with his cuff links, but the words hung in her throat. Beneath the cologne was the familiar scent that was all him—midnight and dark promises and sensual heat.

She remembered the taste of his skin on her tongue, the half promise of heaven, half threat of heartache. The feel of his body wrapped around her. But the sound of his voice? That was all too real. It hadn't changed, not with age and time or education. Not any more than the brutal, irrational desire she still harbored for him, desire she'd warred against so long…and lost every battle.

Uncomfortable with the way the conversation was devolving and scared he'd want to talk about the kiss, she faced him and put up her hands. "Enough, okay? Enough."

He crossed his arms over his chest. "Fine. What are you doing out here?"

"I'm the Bar C's vet."

"And?" he asked, rolling his hand in a get-on-with-it gesture.

She hesitated. "If neither Cade nor Ty said anything about this, I'm not sure I should be discussing it with you."

"I own one-third of this ranch, Reagan."

"On paper, yes." Shifting from foot to foot, she let her gaze wander, let it rest anywhere but on him. "But by operational standards, I believe you'd be considered an owner in absentia."

"And how would you know the appropriate legal term?" His voice was lethally soft.

She finally met his gaze. "That's between you and your brothers, Esquire."

"So they called me home to officially shut me out?"

"If that's what you think, what I said earlier about your intelligence in business is wrong. You're dumb as dirt in that arena, as well," she snapped. "How many ways do you have to hear that they need you, Eli, because I'm running out of ways to say it." She sighed in the face of his silence. "Ty either called you home or he didn't. He either asked for your help or he didn't. But consider this, Eli. How often does a proud man go to his knees and plead for help from the one man least likely to give it?"

His visible flinch was followed by a wince as he touched his split lip. "Yeah, well, I don't think Ty and Cade are seeing eye to eye on what they 'need' from me at the moment."

Reagan stared at him long and hard, noting the split lip, the bruise beginning to blossom on one cheekbone, and the ripped buttons on his shirt. "Cade do that to you?"

Obviously watching her for a reaction, he blinked slowly. "What would you say if I told you I ran into Luke and he called me out on kissing you?"

Every ounce of blood left her face. Spots danced in her vision. She moved in slow motion, closing the distance between them and watching detachedly as her fist connected with his unbruised cheek. Observed his chin whip to the side with absolute indifference.

"What the hell!" Eli bit out, spitting fresh blood.

"You don't talk about Luke. Never again."

"I mention his name and you hit me?" The demand hung between them.

She met his angry stare, her own eyes flat. "Luke was killed three years ago."

Eli's mouth worked silently before he managed a gruff response. "Oh, shit. Reagan, I—" He reached for her, but she waved him off.

"Don't." She spun away and moved stiffly toward the nearest bunkhouse. Her voice hollow in her ears, she called back to him. "Tell Ty I'm taking a few men and heading out to pasture twenty-one."

She battled against the urge to turn back to Eli, to lose herself in the comfort of his arms and the heat of his touch like she had all those years ago. The moment she'd recognized him in Tucumcari, she'd known with perverse certainty that nothing had changed. Eli had left her, broken her heart and left it an empty muscle, but his brand was still there, clear as day. She craved the sound of his voice, wanted his body against hers again and had the strongest…*need* to lose herself in him one more time.

But with Luke's death hanging between them, it seemed as if it would be the ultimate betrayal of the man's legacy. Luke had deserved better than she'd afforded him in life, and she hadn't been able to give it. She'd damn sure try to do a better job after his death, no matter what her heart wanted.

EVERYTHING IN ELI had rebelled at Reagan's admission. He crossed his arms tighter over his chest to hide its shaking and leaned against her truck.

She'd stared at him with that achingly familiar face, those stunning green eyes, her lean body backlit by the late-summer sunshine, and he'd realized she was as familiar as the landscape—and just as foreign.

Everything he believed about her had shifted when he'd discovered she was married. She'd stood up in front of God and everyone and committed her life. *To someone else.* But he'd said it himself—it had been fourteen years. Expecting her to wait when he'd given her no hope had been a kid's dream. No more.

Yet, here he stood with every belief he had regarding Reagan changing all over again. He wanted to ask how Luke had died, but the words stalled deep in his chest. Death wasn't so uncommon out here, but communities were small enough that losing one of their own was like losing a family member. And Luke had definitely been one of the community, their charmed favorite who'd never done anything wrong. Hell, he'd even got the girl.

Guilt swamped Eli at his disrespectful thoughts and he shoved off the truck.

"I've got to get my stuff inside," he said to her retreating form. The urge to run, fast, hard, far, to push every physical limit he had, to go and go until he collapsed made his skin twitch and his muscles tighten even as his breath came shorter. He needed to get away from here. From her. He waited until he was sure his legs wouldn't give out and then started for the house.

"Fair enough. I need to get the herds sorted as soon as possible. Tell Ty I'll have the walkie-talkies."

Eli stopped but couldn't bring himself to face her. Instead, he focused on keeping his voice steady. "What's going on, Dr. Matthews?"

Her breath might have hitched, but it could've been wishful thinking on his part.

She cleared her throat. "Ty really didn't mention anything to you?"

"Apparently there are a lot of things Ty didn't mention to me."

He tipped his chin to his chest, ignoring the emotional hole rapidly unraveling in his chest. All of this—hurt, anger, regret…sweet heaven, the regret—was brought on by the simple sound of her voice, husky and made for whispers in the dark. "If it can wait, I'll just get the news from him." Cowardly, maybe, but too much had happened since he landed in Tucumcari, and he was pretty damn sure he'd reached his breaking point.

She hesitated. "I'm pretty sure it can't wait."

"That bad?"

"Yeah. I'm afraid it is."

Closing his eyes, he gave her profile, just enough that she'd know she had his attention.

"Look, Eli, there's not an easy way to say this. The Bar C is facing quarantine."

Muscles across his shoulders tightened. "Pardon me?"

"You guys may have contracted Shipping Fever on a broad scale."

"Shipping Fever?"

"Bovine Respiratory Disease—temp over 104, nasal discharge, dull eyes, diarrhea, stumbling about, muscle wasting. You've been gone more than a decade, Eli, but I'm sure you remember how the disease appears and what it can do to a ranch, or even a region, if it's not contained."

He blew out a hard breath, ignoring the barb. "How'd

the Bar C herds come down with it? It's the wrong time of year for Shipping Fever. All the stocker cattle should have arrived months ago."

She lifted one shoulder in a shrug. "The ranch recently bought some new replacement heifers of its own. Then there are the late stockers taken on. With the drought and prices high as they are, the ranchers who *do* have grass can feed through the winter and demand premiums. It's messed up the delivery schedules as stockers and feed yards vie for the best growing environment for their steers." She chewed on her bottom lip for a second and then continued. "Everything that came onto the Bar C had health papers—I checked them all— but logic says the disease somehow originated in the new heifers. If it originated with Bar C's stocker cattle, that's one thing. If it's because of the ranch's new stock…"

She didn't finish, but Eli didn't need her to. If the Bar C's own cattle had infected those they'd been contracted to put weight on through the year, the liability would destroy the ranch. The ranch would be quarantined. The cows that didn't die wouldn't do well this year. That meant low revenue. Worst-case scenario would be a huge die-off that would force the ranch to compensate the brokers and owners for the casualties. That would permanently shutter the Covington operation.

He gave a single nod. "I'll tell Ty where you'll be. Four-wheelers or horseback?"

"Horseback. I want to keep from spooking the herd any more than necessary. I'll take one of Cade's horses. We'll trailer them as far as we can to save time, and we'll ride on from there."

Eli nodded and she walked away without another word.

He grabbed his travel bag and then took the porch

steps two at a time. Pausing at the door, hand resting on the iron doorknob, he hesitated. Then he depressed the lever, the door swung in and nostalgia claimed him, reeling him across the threshold like the catch of the day.

The inside of the house still smelled like lumber, wood smoke and leather. Wide-planked floors were scuffed and marked by age and heavy use. His old man's recliner still sat in the corner as if waiting on Max himself to pull up a seat at the end of the day. Curtains his mother had made still framed the window, threadbare with time. A pellet stove had replaced the archaic pot-bellied beast in the stone fireplace. Leather sofas and club chairs were scattered around the room in a haphazard way that announced "bachelor pad" as efficiently as did the abandoned boots near the door and the boxers on the coffee table.

Eli wove through the room and down the hallway to the stairs. Taking a deep breath, he opened the basement door. These he took one at a time. The air was cooler with a bite of dampness to it. He used to love it, especially in July's heat. Breathing faster, he crossed the family room and stopped outside a familiar wooden door. Twice he reached for the handle only to stop. It was stupid, really. Nothing on the other side of the door changed anything about who he was now.

He traced his fingers over the rough-hewn pine door. How many nights had he spent in this basement? How many nights had he sworn that he'd find his way out of a life that had never fit him no matter how he twisted or stretched it as he tried to fill his old man's expectations? How many times had he imagined how fulfilling it would be to make it on his own and *force* his dad to be proud of him? The answer was the same for every question: too many.

On a sigh, he shoved off the casing and stood. One silent twist of the doorknob and the door swung open without a sound. His past crashed into him. Shallow shelves held trophies from FFA and 4-H and high school sports. Laminated newspaper clippings were tacked to a small corkboard exactly as he'd left them. His bed was made. That was different. Looking closer, he realized the room was clean. No dust, no cobwebs, nothing out of place. He was suddenly nineteen all over again and awkward with it. All of the familiar, unwelcome insecurities were still there, waiting, still unresolved after all these years.

Crossing the threshold, his heart stopped. There, on his nightstand, was his favorite picture of his mother. She smiled out at him. Even though her dark hair had been burnished by sunlight in the picture, time had faded the effect. Still, he could remember the way she appeared. The love on her face still radiated from the photo, though. In spades. The years had passed, indifferent to his family's grief at the loss of her, but not even time could change how much Eli'd loved her. Nothing could.

He traced the face in the photo and imagined he could still hear her puttering around upstairs. "I miss her, too."

Eli dropped the picture and the glass frame shattered. "I—" He glanced at the picture and back to the door, where a large man filled the doorway. "Tyson?"

"I don't remember her as well as you and Cade, but it was still hard to lose her."

His youngest brother was now definitely not the littlest. He was a couple of inches taller than Eli's own six feet two inches and clearly comfortable in his skin as he moved into the room. "Grown a bit since you last saw me."

Backing up, Eli stepped on the broken glass and winced at the sound.

Tyson paused, his brows winging down. "What the hell happened to your face? You look like someone dragged your ass down the runway. You do know you're supposed to stay *inside* the plane until it comes to a complete stop at the gate, right?" He snorted. "And here I figured you were the debonair, well-traveled brother." Stepping across the small room, he wrapped Eli in a rib-cracking hug. "It's so good to see you, man."

Eli wasn't sure what he'd expected from his little brother, but given the brutal reception he'd gotten from everyone else, it definitely wasn't this.

He wanted to hug Ty back. He wanted to put distance between them. He wanted someone to shock his heart back into a normal rhythm.

Instead, for just a second, he reveled in a brother's love.

REAGAN AND THREE of the ranch hands trailered their rides as far northeast as they could go on the Bar C. Unloading at the gate to the last pasture on the place, she tossed walkie-talkies to each man and left one in the truck in case Ty or Cade showed up and needed to contact them. Mounting one of Ty's geldings, she adjusted her stirrups and checked her saddlebags. Everything was there, from medical supplies and antibiotics to a pistol for animals that were suffering and beyond help.

Coiling her rope and securing it to her saddle, she whistled for Brisket and headed for the gate. The dog slipped in close, trotting along to keep up.

The men followed in a tight group. Jake Peterson, the most seasoned of the men and another childhood friend of hers, moved up beside her. "How far out do you think the cows'll be?"

She glanced at the midafternoon sun. "I'm hoping we find them in the front half of this pasture. If not, it'll mean getting a chopper out here to push them toward us, and that's not cost effective. It'll also stress them out more than they already are. We'll save it as a last resort." Leaning forward, she tightened her saddle's cinch without stopping her horse. "Regardless, we've got to do whatever it takes to get this contained, Jake."

He settled his hat more firmly on his head and frowned. "This is going to be bad, Reagan, isn't it?"

"Let's not borrow trouble," she said softly, eyes on the horizon.

"No need to borrow when the coffers are full."

She snorted. "Aren't you a bundle of joy today?"

"Just worried. Forgot my canteen. Be right back." He wheeled his horse around and galloped off.

The soft voices of the other men around her and the methodical clop of horse hooves were almost carried away by the sound of the wind whispering through the grass. Being out here on horseback with nothing but the sky above her and the power and potential of one of Ty's cutting horses beneath her proved spiritually cathartic. She hadn't realized how much she'd truly needed the privacy to process the day's events.

Never in a million years would she have suspected today would be the day she ended up facing off with Eli Covington. So much history. So much hurt. She had no idea how she was going to survive the next week or two as she did what she had to do, and he did the same. He'd want the estate probated as quickly as possible.

That made sense. But if this was truly Shipping Fever, it was the worst case she'd ever heard about. She'd have to get the state vet involved.

Wanting more distance, she urged her horse into a swift lope. No doubt the men would catch up, but she'd have a few minutes to herself to just breathe. She never expected the tears that first caught up and then overran her.

Leaning over the saddle, she spurred the horse into a dead run. Ghosts of the past chased her across the plains, nipping at her heels. Their teeth had been finely honed on the sharp clarity of memories she'd once cherished and now resented. Every touch, every kiss, every promise they'd made—every promise they'd broken—it all rushed over her in a ruthless barrage of brilliant recollections. But the taste of him today… It had broken the fragile levee she'd finally managed to build to keep her feelings contained.

The wind whipped her hat off her head. She didn't slow down. If anything, she urged her horse faster, then faster still. Giving him his head, she buried her face in his mane and just held on. A harsh sob escaped as years of blinding heartache flooded through her.

Hoofbeats thundered up behind her. Sitting up, she scrubbed one hand over her face and fought to catch her breath. No one would say anything, but there would be curiosity. And out here, curiosity led to speculation, which led to probabilities, which led to the birth of the most insane gossip. She didn't want to suffer through it. Particularly not with Eli in town.

It had been bad enough when Luke had died. For months, all she'd heard were condolences. The sentiments had been heartfelt, yes. But they'd all been as empty to her as her bed had been at night. No casserole, phone call or sympathy card could take the place of the man who had loved her for five years. She'd learned to hear the words without listening, without assigning them value.

A broad hand reached for her reins.

Sitting deep in the saddle, she parked her feet in the stirrups and shut the horse down. Like the brilliant athlete he was, the horse sat on his hindquarters and slid to a hard stop. Barely winded, he righted himself and stood waiting, ready.

Ty spun his horse and trotted up to her, her hat in hand. He offered the Stetson without comment.

She accepted it, absently reshaping the brim.

"You were running as if the hounds of hell were hot on your heels." Reaching out, he grabbed her wrist. "I checked. No hounds. What's going on?"

Her smile was wobbly as she drew a deep breath and blew out hard enough to puff her cheeks. "I'm good." When he arched a single brow, she nodded quickly. "Honest."

"Don't ever bullshit a bullshitter, Reagan. What happened?"

The noise that escaped was half laugh, half sob. "I thought, just once, I'd indulge myself and try to outrun a past I can't seem to escape. That's what happened." Slapping her hat on her head, she realized the group was quickly catching up. She glared at Ty. "Not a word, Ty. Not to anyone."

"You should probably know that I, uh…" He tugged at his collar and whipped his head to the side, popping his neck.

"Know *what*?" she asked with a snarl.

"That he brought me along." Eli had stopped several feet away, his eyes hidden by reflective sunglasses. He'd changed into jeans and a pair of beat-up boots she recognized from years past. His shirt was clean but wrinkled.

"Great." *How much had he heard?* Whatever it was, she couldn't take it back. Instead, she stared at the very man she'd so wanted to avoid. "Been a while since you've sat a horse, Eli. Do your best not to fall off, would you? Earlier, it seemed you'd already taken the opportunity to roll around in shit. Once a day is our limit out here."

Tyson barked out a laugh. "You rolled around in shit? Where was I?"

Eli never took his eyes off Reagan when he answered. "You missed Cade taking it upon himself to reintroduce me to his fists."

Ty sobered instantly. "So you didn't jump from the plane?"

"No." He shook his head, his eyes still on her. "While I'm flattered you're worried about my well-being, don't bother. I can take what you dish out, Dr. Matthews."

Ty sobered instantly. "That's right. She said you knew about her marrying Luke and—"

"The marriage. Nothing more, Ty, and I insist it stay that way." Reagan reined the horse to the side with a heavier hand than necessary. The animal protested by tossing his head and crow hopping. She settled him down and pointed him toward the northeast again. "Chances are, the herd has holed up out here where they can be sick and miserable without human intervention. I want to get to them as quickly as possible. Either keep up or go home, Esquire."

"You've gotten bossy as hell," Eli muttered.

"And you've got a great manicure. Your point?"

Ty bit his lip and nearly choked on his laughter.

"You always were a smart-ass." Eli coiled his rope

with a practiced ease that made her fight the familiarity of him. "Some things never change."

Settling her hat tight, she forced herself to calm down or she'd transmit her tension to her mount. "True, but some things, and people, do. Don't pretend to know who I am anymore, Eli."

Clucking at the gelding, she slipped into an easy lope.

The sooner she got this job over with, the sooner she could get home and start piecing her life together again. But after Eli's reappearance, it was going to take more than all of her life experience and surgical skill.

It was going to take a miracle.

5

ELI'S LEGS WERE sore by the end of the first hour. By the end of the second, he wasn't sure he still had an ass. He shifted in his saddle as Ty reined in next to him, a wicked smile decorating the kid's face.

"You ever do those *Buns of Steel* videos?"

The casual inquiry caught Eli off guard. "What? No. Why?"

"I was thinking I might market a cowboy version, *Buns of Leather.* You know—ride 'em rough, ride 'em tough, fifteen minutes is never enough."

Eli laughed out loud. The ranch hands glanced their way before casually returning to their own conversation. They'd extended due courtesy to Eli. Their words and behaviors stopped long short of respect, though. To Ty, on the other hand, they were deferential. It chafed.

Ty caught him shaking his head. The youngest Covington reached over and punched the elder in the shoulder. "Give them time, Eli."

"Time to what? Drown me in the stock tank? Drop a branding iron in my lap? Dump my ass in the bull pasture before they take off with my horse? No, thanks."

"I'd forgotten Cade and I did that your last summer

at home. Dad was pissed." His mouth twitched. "If it makes you feel any better, the bulls are on the south side of the place now."

Eli shook his head. "You guys almost got me killed."

"Never saw a guy climb a windmill so damn fast."

"I was up there overnight!" Reaching out, he flipped his little brother's hat off his head.

Ty caught it before it hit the ground, grinning. "And you're still whining about it."

"Shut up." Eli smiled through the grumbled command. In a weird way, it hurt to remember the good times. He'd spent so many years hating who he'd been and where he'd come from that looking back with affection felt wrong, like a betrayal of who he'd fought so hard to become. Being reminded that it hadn't all sucked...it stung.

Then there was the little bit he'd overheard of Reagan's admission to Ty. That more than stung. Way more.

Clearing his throat, he twisted in his saddle and found her. She rode among the men with the surety of one who belonged. He envied her the ease with which she fit in. She'd always been that way, though, so confident and aware of where she belonged. He'd had to scramble to keep up, always feeling one step behind.

Her eyes met his.

A shock of awareness burned through him. He twisted around so quickly he nearly unseated himself.

"She's an amazing woman," Ty said softly.

"Always was." The admission scraped at emotions that were already raw. He adjusted his sunglasses. "When did she marry?"

Ty slouched in his saddle. "Eight years ago."

So long. "Any kids?"

"No. They never—"

A sharp whistle interrupted the conversation. Brisket streaked across the field toward a small cluster of weanlings that had just topped the rise. A second whistle stopped him short. The dog focused on the herd and waited for Reagan to direct his next action.

Eli jerked his chin toward the Border collie, watching as Reagan sent him wide. "She's good with him."

Reagan spread the cowboys out. "Bring these in slow. We'll get them pointed toward the working pens and walk them in. Don't rouse them."

"C'mon," Ty said, heading in the opposite direction of the other three hands.

Eli followed along, his gaze constantly roving as he watched for more steers. Pushing closer to Ty, he considered the black calves with their white faces. "What are you guys running now?"

"Bar C's running all Angus cows. The Charolais bulls provide hybrid vigor and give us the black baldies. Market's still paying a premium for them." Ty jerked his chin toward the little cluster of black steers with white faces. "Those are some of ours. When it comes to stocking, we'll contract anything brokers have and we'll grow 'em out and put weight on 'em for the fall sale ring, provided the price is right."

"Who's running the ranch now that Dad's gone?"

Eli watched the weight of responsibility age Ty a good ten years.

His little brother glanced over and shrugged. "We're managing."

Before he could ask who constituted "we" in Ty's books, one of the steers broke free and headed for the hills. Eli simply reacted. Laying his heels to his horse, he loosed his rope. Someone shouted something after him. He didn't slow down.

Wind whistled past his ears. His eyes watered. The hammering of his heart competed with his horse's hooves pounding the turf. Shaking out a coil of rope, the horse put him right on top of the runaway. Eli's movements were effortless, remembered—as if his muscles had never forgotten. He swung the rope with fluid wrist rolls and watched for the right moment to snag the calf. One swing, two, three—and the horse shut down.

Eli's reaction was a matter of total self-preservation. Dropping the rope, he pushed up on the pommel and vaulted the saddle horn before his junk was relocated into his spine. Over the horse's neck, he ended up straddling the beast's head. His legs clamped around its jaw. The animal backed up rapidly. Eli stumbled forward and rolled, landing flat on his back staring at a stunning blue sky just beginning to turn pink toward the west.

Ty reined his horse in and hit the ground running. "Eli!"

All he could do was weakly hold up a hand.

"Bro, are you okay?" Ty slid to his side on his knees, his hands roaming over Eli as he searched for injuries.

"Me? I'm fine. But my nuts are so damn traumatized they've entered the Witness Protection Program and are passing as acorns."

Ty winced. "I'm not checking your nuts."

Eli rolled his face toward his brother. "That would be bad touch, Ty. Bad touch."

His brother's mouth curled up at one corner. "Your sunglasses didn't fare so well, either."

"No?"

The younger man held up half of the frame, sans lens. "Nope."

"What the hell made the horse balk?" Eli groaned as he sat up, running a hand across his chest and stretching muscles that were grumbling now but would be flat out protesting by sunset.

Ty shrugged. "He's a roping horse."

"So?"

"He put you where you needed to be. Gave you your three swings before he shut it down."

"That's insane. Horses don't count." Eli glanced around and was less than thrilled to discover said horse headed in the direction of the truck and trailer.

"Yeah. Well, around here, we train 'em with pixie dust so they do. Count, that is." Ty rubbed his upper lip. "You, uh, crashed—" a rich laugh broke free "—rather spectacularly."

"Points for style?"

"Definitely. Some free advice, though?" Ty offered Eli a hand up. "Next time try to stick the landing."

"No 'next time,' thanks." Hands on his hips, he stared at the ground. "Cade'll be sorry he missed my humiliation. Listen, I've got to catch a ride to the truck. I'll mend any broken gear and get back out here to help."

"No need." Ty vaulted into his saddle.

It was only then that Eli realized how sore he really was.

"Grab a ride with Doc Matthews while I get the boys to try and regather the calves."

"Ty, I'm not going to—"

But Ty had already taken off, calling the men along with him.

Eli caught the furious look on Reagan's face. Yanking her horse around, she galloped up to him and slid to a stop, no doubt purposely positioning the gelding inches from Eli. "You lost them all."

"If you want to beat on me, you're going to have to take a number, Reagan. It's been a really crappy day."

Her gaze flitted between him and the retreating men. "Go on," he muttered. "I'll walk."

"You'll spook the herd." She tilted her chin toward the cattle that had crested the nearest hill to check out the commotion. With a heavy sigh, she kicked her foot out of the stirrup and hooked her leg over the pommel as she offered him her hand. "Get on. I'll take you to the truck. You can wait for us there."

Eli crossed his arms over his chest. "I'll walk."

"Unless you're the Pied Piper, get your ass in the saddle, Covington. With you on foot, the calves will *never* come in. I won't debate means and methods with you. If we can get these steers into the pen tonight, it means I can test them sooner."

He opened his mouth to argue.

She whipped her hat off, her long brown hair tumbling past her shoulders. "Get on before I give in to the urge to hog-tie your ass and drag you to the truck."

Scowling, pride bruised and ego down for the count, Eli climbed up behind Reagan. His thighs molded to hers and he fought to ignore the fire that burned through him at every point of contact. The horse sidestepped. Eli settled his hands on her hips for balance.

She jerked and twisted away as if pained. "Don't touch me." Her voice was low and harsh.

"How do you suggest we make it to the truck without touching?" Her whole body tensed, and he wondered if she'd jump ship and catch a ride with one of the other men.

The idea of her pressed intimately against anyone else made him grind his teeth. He tried reminding himself she'd been married, but that only conjured images of her and Luke locked in each other's arms. His fingers dug into her hips.

"I said 'don't touch me.'"

Settling his hands on his thighs, he leaned away from her and closed his eyes. "Just get me to the truck, Reagan."

The pain was intensifying, and he suspected the worst of it had nothing to do with hitting the ground.

REAGAN WAS MISERABLY aware of Eli's body, from the way his thighs molded to hers to the way his chest kept brushing against her back, his movements in sync with the horse. How many times had they ridden this way? It might have been a hundred years ago, but the heart didn't forget. She wanted to relax into him, have his arms settle around her waist. Let her head fall into that spot between his neck and shoulder where she fit so well.

"Hold on," she muttered, shifting her weight forward. The horse slipped into an effortless lope.

Eli's fingers brushed her ass as they gripped the cantle.

She moved farther forward, nearly standing in the stirrups. This had been an epically miserable mistake. And Ty? She was going to kill that man. Her mind wandered to the contents of the saddlebags Eli straddled. Maybe she wouldn't kill Ty, but she might shock him with a cattle prod. Maybe grab the tattoo pliers and leave him a more permanent token of her appreciation. Her grin was feral, but she'd never follow through with it. They kept up that pace for more than half an hour, her mind working the entire time.

Eli leaned into her, his chest rubbing against her back. "Slow him down."

She touched the reins and the horse slowed to a walk,

blowing softly. The trucks were just over the next hill. "What's wrong?"

"Nothing. He's getting tired." His voice moved around her, a promise of things long past, his breath skating across the bared skin of her neck. Warmth radiated from him and seeped into her.

Being with Luke was never this good.

And she hated both men for that fact.

Fisting the reins, she stopped the horse. "Get off."

"What? We're almost there."

"Get. Off."

He slung a leg over and slid down, grunting as his feet hit the ground. "What's your problem?"

She shrugged. Guiding the horse with her knees, she pointed him deeper into the pasture only to find the herd cresting the hill. *Damn it.* If she rode toward them now, she'd scatter them all to hell. Instead, she retrieved her saddlebags, slipped off the horse and handed Eli the reins. "Man the gate." Digging through one pouch, she retrieved two cattle prods. Flipping the wands open, she switched them both on before tossing him one as he settled into the saddle.

He fumbled it and managed to shock himself before gripping the handle. "Damn it!" Glaring down at her, his face clouded with thunderous fury. "How long are you going to punish me for doing what you knew I had to do, Reagan?"

Staring at him, her heart stopped. For years she'd dreamed of this opportunity, this chance to tell him what he'd done to her. That moment had arrived, but the words wouldn't come. There were too many variables. She didn't want to hear that she'd been part of what he'd needed to escape. He might respond by explaining to her he'd had to experience life without her. Or he could say that he'd never loved her.

She had only survived this far because she didn't know how responsible she was for his never coming home. Would that change if she did? It wasn't worth finding out.

Stepping away and cursing herself for being a coward, she said the only thing she could. "I don't imagine you'll be around long enough for either of us to find out." Spinning on her heel, she strode toward the working pen. Her tight grip on the cattle prod's handle pressed its checkered pattern into her palm. A sharp whistle brought Brisket to her. Before he stopped, she redirected him with a sharp "Away." Swinging wide and crouching low, he moved counterclockwise as he trotted around the approaching cattle.

Reagan swung the gate open and moved out of their path. Listless and wheezing, the yearling steers moved into the portable corrals with stumbling steps and zero protest. Not good. One calf stood apart from the others, head hanging low. He was gaunt, his sides drawn up. Pointing at him, she whistled for Brisket. "Push 'em. Easy."

The dog slipped into the pen and began weaving back and forth as he herded the steer toward the chute.

"To me," she called as she shut the gate behind the young animal, and Brisket came to heel.

Scrutinizing the black-bodied, white-faced steer, she knew what she faced. From the cowboys' silence, they all did. Didn't matter. She had a job to do. Digging a thermometer out of one saddlebag, she donned a pair of nitrile gloves. Slipping the thermometer into the calf's rectum, the digital readout stopped and beeped at 105 degrees.

The calf coughed—a deep, rattling sound—and stumbled forward a step before going to his knees.

Her arm was caught between the panel and the calf's hip. She yelped involuntarily.

Movement in the corner of one eye said someone was moving in to help.

"Don't," she snapped. "Brisket, bite."

The dog raced around to nip at the calf's heels, forcing him up.

Reagan pulled her arm back, massaging the spot that would be black-and-blue by dawn tomorrow. "Get him into the trailer. There's no point waiting on the results of his blood work. He's not going to make it until tomorrow. I'll put him down when we get to the house. Ty, you'll need to get his information—originating ranch, transport papers, other cattle he's been exposed to here—while I do the necropsy. I'm going to go ahead and say y'all should treat the entire ranch with a broad-spectrum antibiotic that'll address all three major bacteria that could be involved."

Ty shoved his hat back and cursed as he leaped from his horse. "Damn it, Doc, we can't afford to treat every last animal."

She glanced over her shoulder, working to keep her face neutral. "You don't have a choice if you want them to survive. The alternative is letting this run its course, but it's going to cost you a hell of a lot more in death loss and potential lawsuits than if you do the right thing now."

"What's it going to cost, Dr. Matthews?" Eli slipped from the borrowed horse and moved to stand beside Ty.

"You've got, what? Fifteen hundred head contracted and another five hundred of your own? I'm going to guess your yearlings are averaging 900-plus pounds each at this point. On Draxxin, that'll run about $21 per animal. Then we'll be required to monitor them for at least five consecutive days, which means additional feed and, for each group, draining and cleaning out water tanks and hauling off the waste. That's your best…no, that's your *only* hope of getting this cleared up."

Eli stormed forward, his jaw set and eyes hard. "Damn it, Reagan. You're talking about eating up every last penny of profit the ranch might see from its own animals this year, not to mention destroying our relationship with clients when we disclose to them they're facing negative net gains for the early sale ring. They'll have to leave the animals with us longer to make up for their losses, and that costs everyone money. Our pastures will be overgrazed and we'll have to take a full season off next year to allow the pastures to recover. That means everything, and *everyone*, goes hungry this winter *and* next."

She nodded once. "It's not about cost, Eli. It's about stopping this before it becomes an epidemic." Taking a deep breath, she steeled herself for the impending storm her next words were going to bring. "Until then, I have to notify the state vet we've got a BRD outbreak. The Bar C is quarantined."

6

ELI STORMED AND STEWED, his temper tangling with common sense as he worked to fix the tack he'd broken in his "equine dismount." He refused to use the word "fall" because he'd been freaking *ejected* from the back of that horse like his ass was a gymnast and the saddle was a springboard. Despite his irritation, he snorted. Ty would get a kick out of that comparison, and a small part of him breathed easier to realize he knew one of his brothers at least a little.

The cowboys were quiet as they penned the herd and loaded the sick steers into the trailer. They'd push the healthy cows toward the main corrals at the house so Reagan could treat them and begin watching them for the next few days. Once these were treated, the cowboys would begin working through the rest of the herds as they waited on the state vet's arrival. This was about to get very, very expensive.

The horses weren't at risk from the steers' BRD, but the steers could easily have additional complications or infections that *would* affect the horses, so someone would trailer the steers to the main house and corrals while everyone else rode home.

Home.

It had been so long since he'd considered this place that way. His gaze rested on Reagan as she took notes and pictures of the sickest of the steers. Her fingertips flew over her iPad screen. She mumbled to herself as she worked, ignoring everything and everyone around her. Including him. Irritated she could dismiss him so easily, he gripped his horse's repaired reins and started toward Ty. "I'll drive the truck."

"I already asked Everett to drive," Ty responded. He twisted to hook his far leg over his saddle horn. His horse dipped its head low and began grazing as if it hadn't a care in the world. "Gizmo and I'll ride the rest of the herd in with the ranch hands."

Eli arched a single brow. "Gizmo? Last I heard you were raising prized cutting horses, not...Gizmos."

Ty shrugged. "I am. His official name is Doc Bar's Dippy Zippy Gizmo, but all the ladies know him as Gizmo."

"He's a stud?" The surprise in Eli's question was undisguised. The horse should've been as high-strung as a runway model during New York Fashion Week. Instead, he was working "sedated Labradoodle chic."

"Yeah." Ty patted his neck. "I want you and Doc Matthews to ride in ahead and tell Cade we're coming in with some sicklings so he...you and he..." He scratched his jaw and force his gaze elsewhere. "Y'all will need to create a quarantine situation."

Translation: kill the sickest of the animals.

Eli narrowed his eyes, gazing hard at his brother. "I'd prefer to drive."

"And you'd also prefer to do anything that allows you to avoid Reagan and Cade." Ty met him stare for stare. "Neither can happen if we're going to fix this, brother.

Best learn whether or not we can work together now, or we might as well put the for-sale sign out by the road."

Guilt twisted Eli's belly into knots a seasoned sailor would have been proud of. He hated that his little brother was right, that Ty had clarity while Eli was blinded by every new revelation.

Ty glanced over his shoulder before jerking his chin slightly in the same direction. "Go easy with her."

Eli looked at Reagan, the hole in his chest beginning to unravel again, slower this time. The destruction was just as devastating. "'Easy' and 'Reagan' don't play well together," he said softly.

"She married Luke eight years ago—"

"I'm well aware of that," Eli bit out.

His little brother shifted in his saddle, and Eli watched some foreign cocktail of emotions—hurt, anger, grief, rage, regret—slip through Ty's eyes. "She married Luke eight years ago," he said again but with a hardness that had been lacking before, "and was widowed three years ago."

Eli moved closer to his brother and kept his voice very low so no one would overhear them. "She told me he died. How'd it happen?"

"Gored by a Hereford. The owner brought the cow to Luke and Reagan with a severe prolapsed uterus. Luke went out to help, got pinned by the chute gate when it failed and the cow broke loose just enough to reach him." Ty swallowed several times before finishing. "Reagan witnessed the whole thing. She tried to save him. Couldn't. The cow had severed some major artery and Luke bled out before the EMTs even got there."

Eli nodded, the movement entirely reflexive, totally numb. "How'd she do? After."

"She's been working her backside off trying to hold

on to the place they'd just bought together." Ty dipped his chin. "Rumor is she's going to have to sell, though."

"Why?"

"She can't manage a place that size by herself. The Russell ranch neighbors her, and they've offered to pick up her place at fair market value."

The skin along Eli's shoulders tightened. "She ought to sell."

"And do what?" Ty demanded, that low, hard edge decorating his words again. "It's the last piece of him she has left."

"She loved him." Eli choked the words out so softly the wind all but carried them away.

Still, Ty heard him. "She married him."

"Same thing." His chest felt as if it had been filled with something highly flammable that began to burn so hot it reduced his insides to ash. *She'd loved Luke.* That meant, at some point, she'd stopped loving *him*.

The trailer rattled as the steers lumbered inside. Everett shut the gate behind him and said something to Reagan. She answered, the other man shook his head and she handed over her pistol. Rancher-speak for *If he's worse when you get home, put him out of his misery.* Compassionate, yes, but killing had always been something Eli struggled with. One more way he'd disappointed his dad.

"A Covington doesn't flinch when he pulls the trigger, boy," the man had snapped the last time Eli had been given the rifle with instructions to use it on a deformed calf.

The memory drew a line of cold sweat along his hairline.

His attention shifted as Ty straddled his horse again. The youngest Covington picked up the reins and, nudging his horse forward, called out, "Let's get 'em home. Doc and Eli will ride ahead and call Cade soon as the walkie-talkie is within range of the base."

Reagan mounted her borrowed gelding without comment and took up the reins to Everett's riderless horse, turning toward the main house that was a good fifteen miles away. She didn't wait on Eli, though, just urged her horse into a swift gait.

Eli caught up without any trouble and trotted beside her until they were far enough ahead of the herd to spare the horses and slow to a walk.

The setting sun burned up the horizon in a blaze of fiery colors. As the colors faded and darkness began to seep in, it seemed to offer nature's equivalent of amnesty to the perpetual breeze. The night went still. Crickets and frogs collected around the streams and creeks they crossed, the chirping and croaking lost to the splash of the horses through the water and the huff of breath as the horses climbed the opposite banks.

Eli had just opened his mouth to say something when a doe and her fawn, spots nearly gone, shot out of a nearby mesquite stand and bounded away, the whites of their tails raised in alarm.

His breath caught. There was an innate beauty to this place he'd absolutely forgotten. He gazed up at the stars. *Man, the stars.* Night hadn't even fully descended, but the sky was bigger than he'd witnessed in years.

"You ever take astronomy in college?"

Reagan's voice startled him enough he twitched in the saddle. His horse sidestepped in response, and he settled the animal down as he hunted for his voice. Clearing his throat, he nodded. "Yeah. It was one of my favorite electives. Took as many classes as I could. You?"

"Same." She sounded indifferent to the tentative link between them. "I missed the size of the sky out here while I was at school."

"Where'd you go?" he asked.

She rolled her head back and forth. "Undergrad at New Mexico State University. Vet school at Colorado State. Did my degrees consecutively, never taking summers off." Glancing at him from under the brim of her hat, her face was as neutral as the color of a hospital wall. "I didn't want to be too far from home."

"Reagan, I—"

"I heard you went to UT-Austin," she quickly interrupted. "Did you get your law degree there, too?"

"Yeah." He settled deeper into his saddle. "I was accepted to Stanford, but there was no way I could afford the tuition."

"I have no idea how people afford colleges like that. I'm still paying off my student loans."

"That makes two of us."

She opened her mouth and then closed it, chewing her bottom lip for a second before speaking so quickly the words ran together. "Are you happy in Austin? Being a lawyer?"

The answer didn't come easily, surprising him. He rolled his shoulders. She didn't press, giving him time to answer or not. It had always been that way between them, with her giving him as much space and time as he required. And he'd abused that. Sorely.

In the distance, a coyote's yip was answered by another's long howl. Then a third voice joined the chorus. The sound—more soulful cry than call—was so bereft that Eli's thoughts slipped back to the loss Reagan had lived through.

Finally he shrugged and answered her question. "It's

given me the sense of accomplishment I always seemed to lack here. I get recognition for my efforts with the firm. In fact, I made partner two years ago—youngest ever."

"Congratulations."

"Thanks." That same tight-skinned sensation returned with a vengeance. "It's an entirely different way of life, but it suits me."

"I appreciate the insight, but I asked if you were happy."

"Happiness isn't the only thing that matters, Reagan." His answer came out far terser than he intended, but before he could apologize, even clarify, she cast him a sideways glance.

Running a hand around her neck, she massaged her shoulder muscles. "I don't want to fight with you, Eli. I don't want to waste even another second hurting. And I definitely don't want our history to derail what's most important now—saving the ranch."

If she'd whipped off her shirt and said, *Take me now, you hot badass*, she couldn't have surprised him more. "That's a big change from kicking me off your horse a couple of hours ago and tossing me a live cattle prod."

She grinned. "Yeah. Sorry about that. Still have a temper." Then her eyes met his and she truly looked at him, the layers of her grief mingling until he wasn't sure how much she regretted him, how much she hated him being here, how much she might miss what they had and how much was the shadow left by Luke's loss.

It didn't matter.

Altogether, it combined to age her soul, to make her ancient beyond her years and leave her bearing a burden of hurt he would never have wanted her to carry.

He felt responsible and would have given anything for the chance to change it.

Eli's breathing increased. Gripping the saddle horn, he nearly came out of his skin when his cell phone rang.

Reagan glanced over at him. "Impressive service."

"Total fluke if the reception at the airport was any indication of what I should expect out here." He dug the smartphone out of his jeans pocket, annoyed to find the screen cracked, the incoming call's number unreadable. Still, no matter who was on the other end of the call, he'd handle it better than he was handling Reagan. "Covington."

REAGAN HALF LISTENED to Eli talk to someone from his office. His entire demeanor changed. He'd been slouched comfortably in the saddle when the phone rang. Now? He sat so straight it was as if someone had shoved a ramrod up his ass. His crisp enunciation and decisive language made him seem more a stranger than he had since he'd stormed out of her parents' barn all those years ago. She'd watched him seize opportunity that night, and now she knew the results.

"Don't count me impressed," she muttered. Clucking at her horse, she put some space between her and Eli.

He'd asked her about the stars. The *stars*. How many nights had they lain in the bed of his old '74 Ford F-150 and counted falling stars? Too many to count. They'd pointed out the little they'd known about the night sky to each other, always finding the Milky Way, always wishing they could see the Northern Lights. Together. They'd wanted those things *together*. But life had other plans.

It shouldn't surprise her that they'd both pursued astronomy in college, but part of her clung to the small similarity, the hope he'd been thinking of her as they stared at the same night sky. Of course, she may have had nothing to do with him taking the classes. Meanwhile, she'd still been living on the hope he'd find what he needed and come back as he'd promised, then they'd pick up where they'd left off. Together.

A short, raspy breath chased the thoughts out like an emotional exorcism. Those dreams were long gone. She had the sneaking suspicion she'd know where to start looking for them, though. Glancing over her shoulder, she considered Eli.

Guilt hit her mangled heart with a one-two punch and followed up with a kick to the proverbial kidney. Luke had always been steadfast, standing by her when people whispered about Eli leaving. They'd intimated she wasn't enough to bring him home. That's when Luke stepped in and openly began courting her broken heart, had fallen in love with her and convinced the shell of the woman she'd become to marry him. Then he'd set about loving her harder than any man should have to love his wife—hard enough for the both of them.

The truth hadn't been lost on Luke, that she had loved him solid and sound, but she'd never been *in* love with him. God, she'd tried. So hard. But at every turn she crashed into memories of Eli she couldn't escape. She'd finally given up, settling for the fact he and all the memories she had of him were woven into the fabric of her soul. If she was going to have any kind of life, she'd have to settle for what she had instead of holding out hope for the one—the life and the man—she'd believed had been meant for her.

Hooves beat against the grassy turf. Eli reined in next to her, settling his horse into a pace that comfortably matched her own.

She slid a glance sideways at him. "Real life calling?"

He nodded and gave an almost uncomfortable shrug. "Some of my bigger clients are anxious to get me back into the office for upcoming litigation."

"Sounds like… Nope. I was going to say 'fun,' but it sounds like hell, actually."

He laughed. "It's life."

"Seems you'd always be pulled in a million different directions, trying to make everyone a winner."

"As I said, it's life."

"Yeah, well, not everyone wins at life." Try as she might to keep the bitterness from her voice, it still seeped through the tiny pauses between each word.

Urging his horse forward, he cut in front of her and forced her to draw up short. "I'm sorry about Luke and doubly sorry for being a complete asshole about it earlier. I had no idea."

She sucked air into lungs turned to stone. But that's exactly what she'd been doing for years, suffocating. Dying slowly from a kind of emotional asphyxiation that she'd finally stopped fighting. She'd given up living, her choices making her the equivalent of a coward, scared of where every quiet night would take her in sleep and what heartache every new sunrise might bring.

Swinging off her horse, she dropped the reins and started across the field to the small stream that ran through the bottom of the shallow valley.

"Reagan?"

Ignoring Eli's call proved easier than she expected. She just kept putting one foot in front of the other. She ignored the haggard sound of each inhale as she fought for every breath. Thick cedar shrubs crowded the stream banks. She didn't pay any mind to the scratchy twigs and branches snagging her clothes, instead pushing through the brush until she emerged at the water's edge. Two large steps forward and she dropped to her knees, the damp immediately seeping through her jeans as the ranch phone tumbled from her shirt pocket into the creek. Too bad. She dug the tips of her boots through the river rock and buried them in the moist dirt. Plunging her hands into the shallow water, she grabbed fistfuls of sandy mud and squished it through her fingers. Something pricked her palm. She ignored that just as she'd worked to ignore Eli.

Unless she found some kind of anchor, she had the feeling she'd break and simply float away. She sought the reminder that this was her reality, and this— kneeling on the edge of the creek with her hands in mud up to her wrists—was all she could come up with. It was a physical connection with the very land that had kept her safely tethered all these years.

But maybe that was the problem, *her* problem— always playing it safe. The last time she'd gone out on a limb and done something crazy, she'd said "I do" to a man she had known she'd never love. The man behind her *now* had been the ghost that chased her whether she was awake or asleep. She couldn't outrun him. And look how that had ended for Luke, a good man who had deserved better than she'd ever been able to give him. Especially the day he died.

Ever since then, life had been about playing it safe and working hard enough during the day that she fell into bed at night in a heavy and hopefully dreamless sleep. The biggest difference since Luke's death? Now two ghosts haunted her—the ghost of what might have been and the ghost of what should have been.

Whatever had pricked her palm dug in. Reagan blinked rapidly. Her reflection was warped in the lazy eddies of the water, her image colored softly by the last of the sun's glow while somehow also paled by the moon's first light.

It was going to be a long, highly stressful night. The next few days didn't promise to offer any relief from the long hours, strained emotions and death. Always death.

A hand settled tentatively on the back of her neck.

She jumped.

The hand tightened, holding her still as deft fingers began to move along the column of her neck. Thumbs dug into the knotted muscles.

A whimper caught in her throat, and Reagan wasn't sure what she wanted, to plead with him to stop or beg him to dig in harder.

As if nothing had changed and more than a decade hadn't passed since he'd touched her, he seemed to understand just what she needed. He dug both his thumbs into the base of her skull and massaged.

Deft fingers moved down to trace the distinct lines of her collarbones and then up until he cupped her chin. Elijah Covington, home again and touching her as if he wanted her. It was everything she'd wanted save for that specter of a love that hadn't been love, a marriage that had been so unbalanced it was amazing it had remained upright at all.

Eli urged her to her feet.

Unfurling her hand, she gasped at the sharp sting. Looking down, she found a mesquite thorn buried in her palm.

"Reagan."

Nothing but her name, an admonishment of compassion. The tenderness in his tone pulled her toward him like a ship toward safe harbor. But she knew what he represented wasn't safety. That voice promised heat, passion and the kind of empty promises made in the dark that would turn to dust at the first touch of sunrise.

And still, she offered him her palm.

With infinite tenderness, he pulled the thorn free. The wound bled, so he pulled his T-shirt off and wrapped it around her hand. "Hold this tight to stem the bleeding."

Her gaze went from his broad shoulders to his wide chest. He was more muscled than he'd been so many years ago, and it was very evident now as he stood with his shirt off, his hand around hers, his bare upper body less than a foot away. A deep valley ran between well-defined pecs. That valley continued lower, carving an admirable runnel between chiseled abs and his external obliques, that fascinating set of muscles that created the V just inside each hip and ran below the waist of his jeans. "Gutters" they'd been called in college before her biology classes.

A faint smile pulled at her lips as her gaze climbed every inch of bared skin with heated appreciation, pausing when she reached his throat. He was swallowing rapidly, and Reagan had to wonder how in the world they'd ended up here, under the starlight with his shirt off, her hand held in his and her desire for him building at an alarming rate. Leaning down, he kissed the pulse point on her wrist. Once, twice, and then his lips lingered, his tongue flicked over her pulse.

She should have said something. It would have been appropriate. But heaven save her, the sight of him shirtless stole her voice, the intimate touch of his lips, innocently suggestive, had rendered her mute. The man was more physically beautiful than she remembered. Years in the gym had made his body a topographical map of feminine delights. And that gesture, that tender kiss, had softened every reservation she had.

Shaking her head, she dipped her chin and closed her eyes, drawing a steadying breath. "Sorry."

"For looking at me?" he asked so gently she glanced up. With infinite gentleness and moving slow enough to give her the chance to stop him, he grasped her free hand and laid it over his heart. Then he wove his hands through her hair and tipped her face back farther. "You never have to apologize for looking at me like that, Reagan. Ever."

"Things are different now, Eli." Her voice shook even as her fingers curled into the thick pad of muscle on his chest, her fingertips registering the hammering of his heart. "We both know it. If we can just get through—"

His hands tightened the second before his mouth came down on hers, all demand and hunger and wet heat that worked her over until she was nothing but one giant, vibrating mass of nerves. Everything ached with wanting him, ached in a way she'd forgotten she could feel.

She dropped his shirt, intent on pushing him away, only to find her hand snaking up his neck and pulling him closer. Every thrust of his tongue demanded her response, refused to allow her to think, gave her no quarter other than to touch him and move with him, to feel the hard muscle under soft skin and to want everything he offered. Everything.

Reagan had missed this ravenous sexual ache. She'd hungered for this fire that branded her, burned her from the inside out and turned her reservations to ash. She had forgotten what it was like to get lost in a kiss. Forgotten what it was to be oxygen to the flame and flame to the oxygen, becoming so intertwined it was impossible to separate the two as they consumed her.

Eli freed one hand from her hair and, gripping her belt loop, yanked her closer.

And God...and Luke...forgive her, she let herself fall willingly into her first love's embrace.

7

ELI COULDN'T BREATHE. Hell, he didn't want to breathe, didn't need air. He only needed this woman. He'd fought so hard to forget the exhilaration of holding her in his arms as she came alive, as she whipped up his emotions like wind to a wildfire, incinerating his common sense. He'd been with other women, had the reputation of a serial dater among his crowd in Austin, but only because no one he'd ever met did this to him. No one else made him burn so damn hot. The best he'd been able to come up with were mediocre conversationalists who translated to disappointing bed partners. The cold memories only made the woman in his arms that much hotter.

Easing them down to the ground, he propped himself on an elbow, his arm beneath her head, his free hand roaming the dips and curves of her body. She'd always been so firm but feminine. Full breasts strained against her T-shirt. The hem had worked its way loose, and his fingertips dipped below the soft, well-worn cotton to find the bare skin of her belly.

She sucked in a sharp breath and, when he flattened his palm on her skin and let his pinky finger slip underneath the waistband of her jeans, her hips came off the ground to meet his touch.

He'd missed her organic responses, the way he could make her mind cloud over and coax her body into uninhibited acquiescence. For so long he'd thought of her, wondered how she'd been and, only now could admit, had missed her.

She whimpered and shifted her hips toward him, a silent demand he love her body. He unbuttoned the top button of her jeans and eased the zipper down. The skin above her practical cotton bikinis was so soft it drew a groan from his chest. Still, he slowed down, gentling his kiss as he nibbled at her lips before dropping his chin and nipping at the soft spot between her neck and shoulder. She tasted of salt and sunshine. Nothing had ever tasted so good.

Twisting her face away, she choked out, "Don't, Elijah. Don't let me think." She wound her hands through his hair and pulled his face back to hers, her kiss hungry and demanding and so damn heartbreaking he was powerless to do anything but give her whatever she wanted. And what she seemed to want, against all odds, was him.

Shifting over her, he settled his hips between the juncture of her thighs. She lifted to meet the hard ridge of his erection and he ground against her, rocking his body into hers as his balls drew tighter and the slow burn began at the base of his spine.

Somewhere nearby, a cow sneezed.

Reagan froze as the voices of the cowboys they'd ridden with carried across the wind. They weren't terribly close, but if Eli and Reagan could hear them, chances were fair the men would be able to hear them—soon.

Shoving and pushing, Reagan scrambled out from

under him, pulling at her shirt and attempting to button her jeans, but her hands shook so badly she couldn't manage.

Eli stood and moved her hands aside gently but firmly. When her hands fell away, he deftly did her pants up, straightened her shirt and retrieved her hat from where it had fallen near the stream's edge.

She took it without a word, refusing to meet his gaze.

Reaching for his shirt, he shook it out and scrubbed the bloodstain in the water until it was nearly gone. When he stood and faced her, she still wouldn't look at him. "You okay?"

"I don't want anyone to know about this," she whispered.

Her declaration stung. "We didn't do anything wrong, Reagan."

Her eyes snapped to his. The depth of despair he saw in her gaze stole his breath and rendered him speechless.

Then she spoke, her every word tearing at his heart. "You'll leave, Eli. It's not a secret, not to you and definitely not to me. Whatever happens between us is something I'll be left to bear, the proverbial scarlet-letter-wearing woman who couldn't be true to the memory of her late husband."

"It's been three years—" he started, but she waved him off.

"Luke is a saint in this county and probably in heaven itself. I'm cheating on him whether he's waiting at home—" she swallowed hard "—or not. What I want, what I've always wanted with you, isn't possible, Eli."

"That's not true," he ground out. "I have no doubt you were a faithful wife. It's not in you to be otherwise, so this damn town and its gossipy residents can go to hell as far as I'm concerned. You're entitled to live your life however you want to."

"And where do you fit in that anymore?" She sighed. "You're going to leave and I'm going to stay and it will be just like it was before, except you know about Luke now and I'm tired of hating you for never coming back."

For me wasn't said, but he heard it loud and clear.

"I wanted you to come with me."

"And that wasn't possible. No more now than it was then." She wound her hair up and settled her hat on her head. "Anyway, it's history now and not worth reliving. We both made our choices. I'm asking you to respect mine. I…"

"But this is our opportunity to make a different choice, to get a kind of—" he threw his hands up in desperation "—a do-over, if you will. We can make the choice to be together now, for as long as it lasts."

"And how long will that be, Eli?" she asked quietly. "How long will it be before you return to Austin, to be the partner in your firm, fighting the good fight in court…and never looking back."

He turned a tight circle and then stepped into her space, pulling her hat off her head and tossing it aside as he gripped her shoulders. "You're asking me to pull out a crystal ball I don't have. I can't predict what will happen with one hundred percent accuracy. The only thing I can tell you with absolute certainty is that this is our chance to see what's left between us, to see if we can salvage what might have been and make it into something that could be." At her startled expression, he rushed on. "I'm not asking you to make any commitments or promises. What I am asking you to do is to willingly explore this…this…*thing* between us while I'm here. We'll take it day by day, you have the option to call stop at any point, and if you do I'll respect that." He moved in closer. "Your body doesn't lie. You still respond to my touch as much as I respond to yours. It's something we, as two consenting adults, want." He brushed his lips over hers. "I want you, Reagan. Tell me you want me, too."

"I can't deny that whatever this thing is between us clearly hasn't burned out." A deep flush spread up her neck and across her cheeks. "If I agree to see you while you're here, anything we do has to be done privately. No dates, no public affection, no behavior that gives anything away." When he started to speak, she glanced up, eyes blazing. "That's nonnegotiable. I'm the one who'll be left to suffer any consequences once you're gone again. I lived through it once. I don't have any desire to do it again."

Shame combined with regret to make his response sharper than he intended. "Are you embarrassed to be caught with me?"

"Not embarrassed, exactly. I just don't want the judgment and speculation about my private life that will inevitably come along with the action."

Not embarrassed...exactly. Well, wasn't that a rousing endorsement. He'd never been the secret lover his partner didn't want exposed. It hurt like hell, and the truth surprised him. "And if someone finds out?"

She took a deep breath and squared her shoulders. "Then I fully expect you to deny it. We're working together to get the Bar C out from under quarantine. You're probating your dad's estate. I don't care what you tell people so long as it isn't the truth. If you can live with that, we can explore our mutual physical attraction while you're in town. No strings attached, no expectations." She paused, looking over his shoulder.

Her next words were almost lost to the fast-darkening night. "No regrets."

He took a step closer to her, his voice low and hard when he spoke. "So you'd what, use me to satisfy some latent sexual urges and then cast me aside?"

She didn't retreat even one step but went toe-to-toe with him, lifting her face to meet his. "Define it however you want, but you either take it on these terms or pass on the opportunity. Your choice." Laying a hand on his arm, she gave a fraction of a smile. "No hard feelings if you don't want to take it."

Oh, he wanted it, all right. But not with those rules. He didn't want to skulk around as if he was something she was ashamed of or what they might find in each other now was something to regret. It never had been. It shouldn't be now.

But he'd take Reagan any way he could get her. If it meant compromising his pride to keep her reputation intact, so be it. If the terms she'd outlined were the only ones she'd consider, if she truly meant he could take it or leave it, he had no doubt which side of the fence he'd be coming down on.

Illicit affair, it was.

THE RIDE TO the main house passed in general quiet. Eli asked a few questions but cast her a hundred curious looks. It was enough to make Reagan want to take back every word she'd said. They had been uttered in a moment of madness. It was the only explanation. Why else in the name of all that was holy would she offer Elijah Covington a short-term affair?

Intimate images of Luke floated to the surface, and it occurred to Reagan that Eli might think it would be acceptable to come to her house so he could…oh, hell.

She couldn't even say it. "To screw your brains out, Matthews," she forced herself to whisper. "To take you every way you can imagine so you burn him out of your system and lay this particular ghost to rest."

Eli looked over. "I missed that."

"It's not worth repeating."

"I'm curious."

"And that should make me a parrot?" she bit out, then sighed. "Sorry. I'm tired. I don't want to have to euthanize tonight, yet it's unavoidable. I'll have to get medical provisions air shipped and start treating in the field. It's going to be hell."

"I figured." He moved his horse in closer. "What do you think the loss ratio is going to be? Realistically, I mean."

She swallowed hard. "If the entire ranch has been affected, if the cows brought in have intermingled, if they've run the same fence line or shared a stock tank? You're looking at a loss ratio of no less than three to ten. It could be worse if the disease has progressed further in different pastures."

"Shit. We can't afford that kind of loss. If Dad didn't keep up the insurance policies, it'll bankrupt the ranch and we'll be forced to sell it either as a whole or to parcel it off in sections." His face paled. "There could be lawsuits."

"There'd be nothing left to claim."

He shrugged, his shoulders seemingly burdened with possibilities. "Depends on how Dad set up the will. I've got to go over it tonight. If the limited liability corporation is in place, we've got some culpability. If it's an S corp, we're better off." He glanced over at her. "How's your place set up?"

"I don't know." She'd been struggling just to make

the mortgage payments and keep up with her own obligations around the place. She'd never checked how the papers had been drawn up. No, that wasn't true. She'd avoided checking it after Luke was killed. It was one more thing to remind her he was gone, one more thing she had to handle on her own. "I suppose I should find out."

"Get the deed and I'll look it over for you while I'm here," he said absently, his mind seemingly a million miles away.

While I'm here, he'd said. Even now, Reagan had to mentally kick her own rear for laying out the terms of their affair the way she had. She knew he'd leave, but found she was already dreading the idea of it. She'd fight to keep this a sensory experience—nonemotional and nonconfrontational. It was the opportunity she had to have in order to get him out of her system. She'd love him and be loved by him one last time. Then she could—probably—move on and—maybe—reclaim her life. She would sell to the neighboring ranch and pick up a—God forbid—small place in town. But she'd make it work. As always.

They crested the hill to find the main house and three bunkhouses ablaze with lights pouring out from multiple windows. Blue lights flickered in several of the windows indicating the men had their TVs going. Laughter rang across the smooth night air, and all Reagan could think was, *That's about to change.*

Cade stepped out on the front porch, some sixth sense drawing his gaze their way. Full night had set in but, backlit as he was in the open doorway, it was easy to see his entire body stiffen at the sight of them riding in together. He skipped down the stairs, his shirt unbuttoned and the top button of his jeans undone. Reagan had a brief moment to thank God for the Covington genes before Cade was striding toward them, as pissed off as a horny bull pulled off a receptive cow.

"What the hell are you still doing here?" he demanded, reaching out to grab the reins of Eli's mount. The horse shied, nearly unseating Eli. Cade kept coming and the horse began backing up rapidly.

"Enough!" Reagan shouted, the command harsh.

Cade spun on her. "No offense, Reagan, but this is Covington business."

"Not anymore it isn't. You've got BRD spreading through your herds."

The middle Covington brother froze and considered her, his voice softer when he finally spoke. "I figured Everett had somehow misunderstood."

"He didn't. Eli and I intended to radio you ahead of our arrival, but I had a small accident—" she held up her bloodied hand "—and I dropped the radio in the water. Regardless, we're here now and we've got to get a handle on the outbreak. A large part of that is going to be you two working out whatever it is between you, so the bullshit stops and the collective priority becomes saving the Bar C. Eli might've just shown up today, but he gets that. He's helped me all evening to sort and gather, and Ty and a handful of cowboys are going to be here soon with the first herd. I'll have to have quarantine corrals set up, chutes to work in, lights for night work and food and drink for the men. The horses will have to be moved, preferably to a pasture nearby or to the barn where the doors are kept closed. I'll treat them with a full-spectrum antibiotic as a precaution for anything else the cows might be carrying, but I still don't want them exposed to any more than they have to be."

Cade's eyes widened. "Did you just dare to insinuate

he cares more about the Bar C than I do?" There was a dangerous undertone to his words.

But Reagan was beyond the point she was willing to play *Family Feud*—Covington Style—with these two. "Out of everything I just laid at your feet, that's what you focused on? Grow up, Cade. I mean it. If I can work with him, so can you. So stop being so self-righteously pissed off over a history that can't be changed and grow a big-boy pair that'll see you through this." She swung down off her horse. "After this is done? You two can kill each other for all I care."

He stared after her as she stormed toward the barn, but she still heard him say to Eli, "Some days I wonder why you ever left that woman."

And Eli's response: "So do I, Cade. Trust me. So do I."

8

THEY WORKED ALL NIGHT, and by the time the sun began to color the eastern horizon, Eli wanted to fall facedown on a bed. Or the hayloft. Or, hell, even a quiet piece of ground where he hopefully wouldn't get trampled.

He'd forgotten the working-all-night-then-pushing-on-to-do-chores-come-dawn thing that came with ranch life. You did what you had to do, and that's exactly why he found himself still in the barn well after dawn, shirt tucked into the pocket of his jeans and flinging hay bales off the giant stack. Several split on impact, and he cursed a blazing blue streak. He'd have to clean those up and feed them by tractor. Obviously, he'd lost his touch. Used to be he could chuck bales off the roofline and get them to land solid. That had been so long ago.

Soft footsteps interrupted his rhythm. Pausing, he peered over the edge of the giant pyramid-shaped hay-stack built into the corner of the barn to find Reagan moving from horse stall to horse stall, vaccination gun in hand. Voice soothing, she'd slip inside, inoculate the animal and move on. Ty went ahead of her to indicate which of the mares were pregnant. Reagan would pull out a different vaccination gun and treat those before going back to the regular dosing.

"Seems like you made up with Eli," Ty remarked casually, opening a stall door for her.

"I guess."

"You guys were pretty in sync all night, pushing cattle, treating the sickies, sorting the rest. It was like old times."

"Not quite, but easier than it could have been."

Ty stroked a mare's nose and looked at Reagan. "What made it easier?"

She shrugged. "I've been angry for fourteen years. That's plenty long for the best of women to carry a grudge."

"A grudge, huh?"

"I chucked the voodoo doll I made in his likeness before we got to work last night. You know, just to keep from backsliding." She glanced at him, the irony in her deadpan stare heavy. "But thanks for trying to help us work it out. At *every* opportunity."

"I didn't—" He coughed, then grinned. "Okay. I did."

Eli remembered enough about Ty to know he'd start badgering Reagan about her ride back to the ranch with him, so, he tossed a bale of hay down the far side of the haystack with such lack of care it split and scattered on impact. Both Ty and Reagan jumped. He leaped from bale edge to bale edge, agilely descending the giant haystack. "Thought I heard voices down here."

"Never took you for one to lurk in haystacks and eavesdrop," Reagan said, her words heavy with censure.

"Not my speed. I heard voices, thought one was yours, so I came down." He forced himself to grin charmingly. "You're not disappointed to see me, are you?" His smile faded as the silence drew out between them. When she only stared at him, his eyes narrowed.

"In the name of self-preservation, I'm out of here," Ty muttered. Snatching up the vaccine gun, he passed it to Reagan handle first. "I don't care what he says, don't inoculate Eli. It'll piss me off."

Both Eli and Reagan glanced at the typically affable youngest brother. The sharp edge to his tone said he was less than amused with her poking at Eli and wouldn't hesitate to give her hell if he had to. When Ty spun on his boot heel and strode to the barn door, Eli saw his opportunity and seized it.

"Do me a favor, bro?"

The younger man stopped but didn't turn around. "What?"

"Bar the barn door for me. Both ends."

Ty's brows winged down. "You remember how to get out?"

Eli glanced at Reagan, who had begun to shake her head. "Yep. If it's anything like riding a horse, I'm pretty damn good at it given all the practice I had growing up here."

One corner of Ty's mouth lifted with humor. "Your reputation could stand a good romp in the hay."

"Yeah?"

This time Ty truly smiled. "It might loosen the stick Austin seems to have wedged up your rear end."

"Get out, asshat," Eli called, flinging a flake of hay toward his brother. "And shut the damn door."

"Getting and shutting." He pulled the barn door closed behind him, the action followed by a heavy *thunk* of the wood baluster that pinned the doors closed from the outside.

Reagan looked up at Eli, eyes wide, dark circles easy

to see even in dim light. "What are you up to, Covington?"

"Making the most of the time we've got for that illicit affair. I intend to start now."

SOMEONE MUST HAVE sucked all the air out of the barn. It was the only logical reason Reagan stopped breathing and couldn't get her lungs to reengage. "What are you talking about?"

"Hey, you were the one who set the terms—secret, right? With everyone out there working and assuming you're in here doing the same, they ought to leave you alone for at least a little while."

"They'll see Ty out there in the corrals," she hissed, backing away from him.

"And he'll cover for us."

"Why? What's in it for him?"

A strange shadow passed over his face, half pain and half relief. "He'll do it because I came home when he asked me to." He closed the distance between them, hooking a finger under her chin and lifting until their eyes met.

Hot and cold, want and regret, desire and worry— they all raced through her, driving her to want to take up drinking. "This is crazy," she whispered.

"I prefer to consider it in legal terms," he whispered in return, stepping even closer.

"Which are?"

"Temporary insanity. It forgives a great deal, and I want you to forgive me for this."

He moved so quickly she didn't have a chance to defend herself. Getting his shoulder into her hips and pelvis, he stood, picking her up like a sack of grain.

"Elijah Covington, you put me down right this second," she demanded, struggling. "Put me down or you're going to find yourself inoculated for a variety of diseases."

Tightening his grip, he ripped a horse blanket off a saddle resting on the hitching post and started up the hay bale, strong enough that he moved with confidence and ease. "Stab me with that vaccine gun and I'll tan your ass, Matthews."

The temptation to see if he'd follow through nearly had her pricking him with the needle, but she managed to refrain. Barely.

Once at the top, he tossed the blanket down, spreading it out by foot before going to his knees and laying her down gently. "Eli—"

"Hush, Reagan. I agreed to your terms of privacy and secrecy. I don't like it, but if it's the only way I can get my hands on you? So be it. I've been here a mere twenty-four hours, and it's been one constant reminder after another that I suck at being a Covington. The only thing that I ever got right in my life before I left for Austin was you. Not even my old man could condemn me for that." His throat worked as he swallowed hard. "You were the only thing that was ever right about this place, the only thing that fit and the one thing I couldn't take with me. I don't want to have to wait for sundown and convenient timing to touch you. Not now. Now when I have you within reach again, baby."

"No pet names."

"That wasn't part of the original negotiation."

Her eyes narrowed. "Consider it an amendment."

"Sorry. Original contracts have been accepted as presented. No more negotiations," he said softly as he untucked her T-shirt.

Her breath came faster as his soft fingertips brushed

her ribs. Then he ran a hand up under her shirt, through the neck and gripped her throat gently. As he stroked her chin with one thumb, her eyes widened. "This is new."

"I left here an insecure boy who couldn't navigate his way through his family's politics. I'm not that boy anymore. I know who I am, know my own worth. I want to know who *you* are now, the type of woman you've become. From what I've seen so far? You're everything I believed you could be and more. Neither of us are the people we were fourteen years ago. We both need to remember that."

His grip tightened momentarily and her back arched hard enough so that only her shoulders and booted feet were in contact with the hay beneath her.

He dragged a hand down her chest, over her sternum, spreading her breasts even as his thumb and pinkie raked over her swollen nipples. She drew in another shaky breath. "And what does that mean exactly, that we're different people?"

His grin was slow. "It means I've wanted this long enough you should probably prepare yourself to hang on tight."

"You've wanted this?" Nerves she'd believed long dead flared hard and fast, and awareness spread across her skin.

Eli's face grew somber, his broad hand resting across her belly. "More than you can possibly imagine. And I have an active imagination where you're concerned." He closed his eyes and drew a breath so deep his chest and shoulders seemed larger in size. When his gaze finally found her, his eyes were so serious.

Her nerves released little butterflies through her body. "Kiss me, Eli."

"As my mistress commands," he murmured, lowering his mouth to hers.

His tongue touched hers tentatively before his confidence surged. The years fell away and everything was familiar in a way that was all new. They devoured each other. Her hunger for him burned through her, a gasoline-fueled blaze.

Every time she thought she'd caught up with him, he'd change the way he touched her, change the angle of his kiss or move his lips to her ear to whisper suggestively as he caressed her body.

Raising her up, he divested her of her shirt and bra before laying her back down with a sort of desperate reverence. His eyes skipped over her, leaping hungrily from point to point before settling on the button of her jeans. Toying with it, he began to say something twice but stopped himself each time.

She pushed to sitting and leaned on her hands. "Something you want to say about my brand of denim?"

"You're more beautiful than I ever remembered," Eli said in a hushed voice.

Her heart stumbled and threatened to take a dangerous fall in his direction.

Reagan could manage sex. She knew she could. But manage him? Never. So she did the only thing she could to keep herself from baring her soul. "You've obviously not been laid in a while if a farmer's tan is doing something for you."

He traced the line where deep tan gave way to pale skin on her arm, that point where shirtsleeve began and ended and left a year-round difference in the color on her flesh. When his gaze finally made its way up to hers, she regretted the quippy remark. So much rested in his stare. From regret to contentment, hunger to anxiety, it was all there.

It made him suddenly, unequivocally real to her. She'd spent the past twenty-four hours knowing he was here, yes. But it had been with the general understanding he was temporary, a passing attraction no more permanent than a traveling circus.

But this ringmaster ran her emotions, putting them through their paces with every proverbial crack of the whip that came in the form of his brand of humor, his charm, his compassion. This combination of him and her was dangerous.

She'd truly believed she could manage this affair. Now she wondered if both of them would walk away from this scarred worse than before.

He unbuttoned her jeans. "What's going on in that mind of yours, Reagan?"

Nothing safe, and definitely nothing welcome. So she lied. "Seems I'm in a bit more of a rush than you are. It's unfair." Hooking a leg around his thighs and an arm around his shoulder, she half flipped, half rolled him over so he ended up on his back with her straddling his hips. His erection pressed against the seam of her sex. She grinned. "Maybe you're more rushed than I thought."

Eli settled his hands on her hips. "I wanted this first time to be more than a roll in the hay."

Her belly flipped over. *This first time.* So this was going to be more than a single occurrence. She had to concur.

Once would never be enough.

9

CLOTHES CAME OFF in a confusing rush, and they both laughed a bit manically when Eli couldn't get one boot off. It took both of them to wiggle his foot free.

Then, suddenly, the laughter dissolved into the kind of anticipatory silence that built before a storm broke. And it would be the kind of storm that leveled outlying buildings and sent both man and animal running for cover. Eli held no false illusions about what coming back together with Reagan would be like...or would mean.

Laying her down on the blanket, he started with her jaw, kissing her tenderly before nipping the soft skin and soothing it again with little kisses, small licks and murmured words of affection and encouragement. He wanted to draw the little noises out of her that drove him wild, evidence he'd done the same, was *doing* the same, to her. She was passionate. She was responsive. She was so alive compared to the handful of lovers he'd been with over the years. Not a one of them could hold a candle to this amazing woman.

He was lost to her all over again, to the smell of her shampoo, the taste of hard-earned sweat on her skin, the musk of her undeniable arousal. She was everything to him in that moment—his sunrise and sunset, every minute of his day and every hour of his night. She was the one thing that had ever been right about home.

Slipping down her body, he pressed her legs open and ran his tongue along the seam of her sex. It thrilled him when her hips bucked involuntarily, lifting her off the blanket.

She cried out.

"Shh," he said, breathing against her cleft.

"Eli," she begged.

He didn't stop. Settling in, he tasted her deeply, reveled in every shudder of her body as he drew closer and closer to her clit.

She moved in fits and starts, trying to force him to get to that magical place that would send her over the edge.

He resisted. At least initially.

Then it was too much—her reaction, her arousal, her unarguable need for him. Dragging the tip of his tongue over her clit, he circled it rapidly, then suckled it. Gently, he built the pressure and at the same time he flicked his tongue over the hard knot.

Her shoulders rose off the blanket as she came. Eyes wild, Reagan bit her lip fiercely. Every breath came fast. She clutched his hair and rode his mouth as the orgasm took her higher, soft whimpers escaping despite her best efforts.

Gripping her wrists, he pulled her hands free of his hair, dug a condom from his wallet and sheathed himself to the root with shaking hands. "Lie back," he commanded softly. "I want to see your face when I take you."

She slumped down, her breathing heavy, her eyes alight with expectation.

He covered her body with his, planting his forearms next to her shoulders and settling his raging erection against her. Adjusting his approach, he gripped his cock. "Spread yourself for me."

She complied.

His heart lodged in his throat. She was beautiful. Perfect. Raising himself up, he settled one hand against the blanket and the other on his rigid shaft. He fed the head into her slowly, shocked at her channel's narrowness, thrilled with how wet she was. He had to take his time—feed in an inch, retreat. Feed in another half inch and retreat.

Then she took control, lifting her hips and taking him to the hilt with a gasp.

He grunted as he hit the end of her channel. She was so tight it almost hurt.

"Move," she commanded, voice straining. When he hesitated, she began to draw herself off him.

"Don't you dare," he nearly growled. Holding himself on his forearms, he used his knees to spread her legs wider. She followed his silent direction, bending her knees more and lifting her hips to meet his thrusts. He began with a slow in and out movement, rolling his hips to insure he covered her G-spot with every entry.

She moaned. "More. Please, Eli. I… I need…"

"What, beautiful? Tell me, Reagan." Shaking her head, she tried to force herself back down his length, but he gripped her chin. "Say it."

"Raw. I want this raw and real." She gasped, pushing against him. "Please, Eli. Please."

And in giving her what she needed, a little bit of him fell into the mix. He fumbled the rhythm when he realized he'd offered part of himself to her, but she couldn't possibly understand, refusing to let him slow down.

Pushing against him, she moaned low but clear. "Yes. Yes, yes, yes."

The unguarded pleasure in her voice pushed aside his intention to make this a matter of gentle lovemaking. Instead, he rode her with increasing roughness, the sound of slick skin slapping slick skin creating the most erotic sound he'd heard in…fourteen years.

She met his every stroke, refusing to let him have the upper hand. She was so different from the gentle lover she'd once been, and he was crazed by the woman she'd become. Her demands drove him higher, made him ride her harder. His fingers dug into her firm flesh as the burn of release began near the base of his spine. "Not yet," he ground out.

Reaching down, he pinned her hips down and shifted higher so he scraped her clit with every drive forward. One stroke, two, three…and she came apart in his arms with a shout.

Curled over her body, Eli rode her harder, his own release bearing down on him with unapologetic force. He came with a shout, gripping her so tight he feared she'd bruise. But damn if he could stop himself.

Slowly slipping down from that precipice of ultimate release, he stroked her pinked skin and ran a fingertip down her neck.

Eyes closed, breathing fast, she managed a small smile.

"What?" he panted as he withdrew and shifted to lie by her side.

"I'm going to go out on a limb here and say that getting to know the man you've become is going to have some serious perks. Unless that's all you've got going on, Esquire."

He rolled her onto her side, following the motion with his own as he draped an arm around her waist. "Not even close, Doc. Not even close."

THE MOMENT REAGAN pulled herself together, she left the Covington place in a cloud of dust. She'd been so worried that everyone could tell what she and Eli had been up to that she'd nearly left Brisket behind.

That had been the litmus test of her emotional well-being. Her life's stability had crashed and burned within twenty-four hours of Eli's return. She didn't even want to think about what that might mean.

Pulling up to her small log cabin, she put the truck in Park and sat staring blankly through the windshield over wide, barbed-wire-fenced fields. Somewhere nearby, a calf bawled, calling for its mother. Reagan could relate. If her mother weren't still so hung up on Luke's memory, she'd give the woman a call and ask her advice. But her mom believed in Luke Matthews's sainthood, and if she suspected her daughter had defiled his memory, let alone with the reviled Elijah Covington, she'd probably have a heart attack. Or a seizure. Or both.

Neither would stop her from condemning her daughter's actions, though, and Reagan couldn't take that. Not right now. But if Eli would hold to his word and keep the affair a secret, Reagan hoped she would never be put in that position.

That was the only downfall to living in such a small town. Everyone took an interest in everyone else's business, and no one hesitated to volunteer their two cents— to your face or behind your back. She hated being talked about. Hated being the object of speculation, be it curious or malicious. Hated that she had to remain above it all in order to keep her business healthy. Her livelihood was contingent on the very people who gossiped about her, and it sucked.

She pulled her hat off and ran a shaking hand through her hair. Brisket licked her wrist, and she turned her attention to him. The dog had never known Luke, but she had no doubt he would have loved the man.

Still, the Border collie's loyalty would have been to her and her alone. It was her gift, building these wordless relationships with animals. It was what had, in part, led her to pursue veterinary medicine. It was also a decent career that had allowed her to come back home with a solid job in the otherwise unstable communities of northeastern New Mexico. No one could leave her or force her to leave. She would be responsible for herself and only herself, and that was exactly what she'd wanted in the wake of Eli's abandonment.

Eli's abandonment.

And she'd just willingly set herself up to be abandoned again. Soon.

Making love with him in the barn had convinced her that having a private affair had been as asinine a choice as her decision to marry Luke.

She'd known she wasn't in love with Luke when he'd asked, but he'd presented her with what seemed to be, even in retrospect, a hundred excellent reasons why they should make the ultimate commitment to each other. He'd told her then he was well aware she'd always love Eli, but he had been so convinced he could make her love him, too. It would just take time, and he was willing to give her that. All she'd needed to do was say yes, to step out of the shadow of history and live in the light of the present.

So she'd said yes.

But what she'd found with Luke hadn't been living. Because it hadn't taken her any time at all to realize Luke *had* been the perfect husband...for someone else. She'd done him the greatest disservice by marrying him.

From the first, she'd tried to be a good wife, to be a companion and responsive lover. She'd never quite pulled it off. She'd believed herself more a fraud every day, the layers and layers of guilt building a thicker and thicker wall between her and Luke. Then he'd died. And those layers, those walls, had become unsurpassable.

Because while she had cared for Luke, had truly loved him in the dispassionate way of a steady, nonsexual companion and had mourned his loss, she'd never been brokenhearted over it. Not like she'd been when Eli left her.

She was a horrible person, and if anyone ever realized the truth about how she'd felt at Luke's death, she'd be shunned as the county pariah. She'd have to leave.

She threw the driver's door open and hit the ground at a run. She made it to the edge of the porch before she lost the meager contents of her stomach.

The problem? No matter where she ran to, she couldn't get away from herself or her past. Eli had proved that with amazing efficiency. A hard shiver skipped down her spine. He'd owned her body this morning, taking her to heights she'd forgotten a woman could reach. And he'd done it with a finesse he'd lacked as a teen. The realization he'd learned to be such an accomplished lover by *being* a lover to other women made her hands ball into fists. It wasn't as if they'd had a commitment to each other, but she'd been faithful to his memory, had held out hope he'd return for her even though his parting words had been so decisive.

"One of these days, I'll be back," he promised gruffly, moving out of reach as he snatched his duffel bag up and hoisted it over his shoulder. *"This damn two-light town will see exactly what I'm made of."*

What she'd heard was that he'd be back.

What he'd meant was things between them were through.

Until now.

Brisket whined from the open door of the truck, waiting her command that would allow him to hop down.

"Out," she said softly.

The dog leaped from the truck and nearly belly crawled to her. Canine intuition told him something was very wrong, but the environment gave no clue as to what it was. Being Brisket, though, and loving her the way he did, he sidled up to her and pressed against her legs.

"It's fine." She stroked his head.

His feathery tail wagged, stirring up the dust.

She climbed the stairs and walked across the porch, pushing into the house and tossing her bag on the seat of the hall tree. Stripping as she went, she crossed the living room and went straight to the shower. The water was hot enough to scald, but it didn't faze her when she stepped under the aggressive spray. She craved the benediction of the cleansing heat. Water sluiced over her head, over her face and down her body.

The one thing she couldn't deny was that being well used by Eli had left her with delicious tiny aches and tenderness. It had been years since she'd had sex. Even more years since she'd experienced desire so raw it left her body demanding more than a creative imagination.

She stepped out of the shower and toweled off, wrapping her hair up and pulling on her T-shirt and boxers.

The answering machine by her bedside blinked, advertising eight messages. They were probably clients. Maybe her neighbors. Regardless, those callers were going to have to wait. She'd been up for more than thirty hours.

Pulling her quilt back, she fell into bed. Sleep crowded her consciousness before she got the towel off her head.

And for the first time since Luke had died, she went to sleep unafraid of dreaming.

10

ELI FELL OUT of his twin bed. Twice. "Damn it," he shouted the second time he crashed to the ground. Surely the bed hadn't been this small when he was a kid. It wasn't possible. He'd have ended up with brain damage. And the carpet-on-concrete floor certainly hadn't softened with age. Irritated, he shoved to his feet and wrestled the covers into place.

The pristine sky shone through the lone window. The sun was high; he needed to get his saddle-sore ass in gear. Besides, the aches and pains he'd earned from yesterday's manual labor meant there'd be no more sleep. The gym was fine for building a body, but hard work revealed muscles a person forgot they had and, despite his exceptional physical conditioning, he apparently had a hell of a lot of those very muscles.

His phone rang and he dug it out of the pocket of his briefcase. The broken screen again scrambled the incoming number but chances were solid it was an Austin number. "Covington."

The voice at the other end came through so garbled he couldn't understand a single word.

"Hold on," he said loudly, as if yelling would help.

Jogging out of the room, he was up the stairs and outside before the signal cleared. "Covington," he repeated.

"Mr. Covington, it's Lynette."

He fought a sigh. Lynette, his paralegal, was the best there was, but she could get a little codependent in his absence. She always had to have more direction on the larger cases when he was out of the office, a bit more reassurance in her decision making. But her output? It was the sole reason she was at the top of her field. She worked circles around the other paralegals once she was set on task, and what she produced was impeccable. Getting her to take the initiative without his approval proved the only challenge.

"What can I do for you, Lynette?"

"Sir, the president of Macallroy Oil is demanding an in-office meeting with you tomorrow at ten o'clock central time. I advised him you were out of the office, but he's insisting you be here to discuss the prosecution's settlement offer." She drew a deep breath. "He's livid, Mr. Covington."

Eli pinched the bridge of his nose. "Explain to him my father passed away."

"That was the first thing I did, sir. He was rather—" she sniffed "—vulgar in his response."

Brows drawn together, Eli couldn't imagine what the old jackass had said to earn his paralegal's disapproval. She'd witnessed and heard plenty to toughen her skin. "Define vulgar."

"I'd rather not."

"And I'd like to know how hard I'll be taking him to task when I return his call."

She took a moment to answer, her voice low when she finally got around to it. "He said he didn't care if you were stuck in the Australian Outback and your dick had been eaten by a dingo. You'd best slap a Band-Aid over your bare balls and get your ass to the meeting or, for what he's paying you, he'd find another lawyer that would make Macallroy Oil his *only* priority."

While it wasn't exactly vulgar, particularly for the man in question, it had offended his paralegal, and Eli took exception to anyone abusing the people he considered himself responsible for. "If he calls in again, tell him I'll be in touch within the hour."

"Should I expect you in the office, Mr. Covington?"

Eli paused, thinking through the logistics. He could theoretically get to Austin today if he left now, but he'd only be able to make a single meeting. Then he'd have to get back here to carry out his responsibilities to his brothers. It seemed pointless, but Macallroy Oil was one of the firm's most profitable clients, and pissing the old man off wouldn't end well for anyone.

Sighing, he closed his eyes and tipped his head to the sky. He usually had no problem prioritizing. But the current demands were all pulling him in different directions, and he didn't know how to manage what everyone expected of him.

In the distance, someone fired the tractor up. Cattle called out at the promise of food, rattling the chains that held the metal gates as they jostled for the best positions at the round bale feeders. Overhead, the sun beat down on his face and warmed his skin.

"Are those…cows?" Confusion infused Lynette's question.

"Yeah." Eli hadn't shared his background with his coworkers. The most anyone at the firm knew, he'd moved to Austin to go to school and had stayed. Nothing more personal ever passed his lips.

"Where are you, Mr. Covington?"

He hesitated. "Taking care of some business." Even now, he couldn't bring himself to reveal his rural upbringing, to admit ties to this place he'd called home for nineteen years.

He'd worked hard to cultivate his image, one of urbane sophistication, not that of an unpolished, dirt-road-driving, tractor-owning cowhand. He rolled his shoulders and ground his teeth.

Shoving a hand in one pocket of his jeans, he forced himself to admit that for the first time, he was ashamed of himself for leaving the ranch and his family as he had. He'd always blamed his old man for not being able to see past Eli's shortcomings. Not once had Eli recognized in himself the longing to be different—he'd just wanted to be "better" than the people he'd grown up with.

He'd dismissed them en masse after his mother died. The lack of civilization had killed her, he'd believed. But in truth? She'd made her place here. She'd been the epitome of class and grace. She'd displayed loyalty and affection, been a good friend and neighbor and more. He'd been the uncivilized one.

He'd been so full of self-righteousness he'd never even tried to look for the good in this place and the people who made it what it was. *Shit*. He'd really screwed this up.

Or being here was screwing *him* up. He'd never questioned his choice to leave, never felt guilty about the man he'd been or the man he'd become. Not until all this emotional bullshit started sticking to his borrowed boots.

"Are you there, Mr. Covington?"

He forced himself to speak. "Yeah. If Macallroy calls, tell him I'll be in touch within the hour. I'll be there for the meeting, but do *not* advertise my availability to anyone else. There's too much left to do with this estate business, so I'll be returning after that meeting."

"Yes, sir. Do you need me to make travel arrangements?"

"No. I've got it. Have a good afternoon." He disconnected and went back into the house, sank into his dad's favorite recliner and used the house phone to call Macallroy.

The old man answered on the second ring. "Don Macallroy."

"Don, it's Elijah Covington."

"So your little secretary managed to reach you? Figured she would if I made it clear I'm prepared to walk."

"Let's not get off on the wrong foot here, Don. While I appreciate your creativity in having me unmanned by a dingo, my father died. There are obligations to the family I have to fulfill."

"Unless those particular obligations fund your bank account, you've got your priorities out of order, Covington. *I* provide the income that allows you to live the lifestyle you do."

"You're not my only client. And my lifestyle and how I pay for it is none of your concern, Don," Eli snapped. He'd intended to keep this entirely professional no matter how the old man goaded him, but Eli's front-porch epiphany had brought too much emotion to the surface. Still…

"Don, I'm trying to work with you here. The best I can offer is a nine o'clock Skype call tomorrow morning. I'm not coming into Austin for a personal meeting, because I have to attend the first probate hearing at the local court by one tomorrow afternoon. That's not negotiable. But I'm willing to work with you remotely to settle whatever has disturbed you."

"You'd better come to the virtual table with some answers, Covington."

"Anything in particular?" The cold edge to Eli's words was unmistakable.

The old man matched his tone. "I want to know what the hell would prompt you to encourage us to settle for $35 million. You're supposed to be on our side in this, but I get the distinct impression Macallroy Oil is getting the shaft, and the bitch isn't using lube."

Eli's stomach pitched as his ethics bucked wildly. His client had run an oil carrier ashore. The hull had been breached and the crude had been dumped into the North Atlantic. Every study conducted indicated the disaster would affect the environment for the next twenty years. He'd proposed they accept this settlement because, if anything, Macallroy Oil should be paying three times the amount. But it wasn't Eli's job to point out his client was "lucky." It was his job to get the bastard the best deal he could. It wasn't the first time he'd been faced with having to do something that went against his personal beliefs. For some reason, though, this particular event chafed worse than ever.

"Conference call at nine tomorrow, Don. It's the best I can do." He barely refrained from adding *Take it or leave it*, with the hope the old man would leave it.

"Mind yourself, Covington," Macallroy said softly. There was a distinctive click.

Eli fought the urge to punch something. He needed to go for a run, lift some weights, throw some hay around—something. It wasn't an option, though. Not with so much to do.

He called Lynette to let her know he wouldn't be

coming in after all, and instead asked her to email him the Macallroy files and arrange the conference call with his fellow attorney on the case, Amanda English, and then Don. He wasn't dealing with the old man without witnesses.

Eli disconnected at the same time Cade came through the front door.

The other man paused, looking him over. "Odd seeing you in Dad's chair. Hell, it's odd seeing you here at all." Then he surprised Eli by moving to the sofa and flopping down. "Damn, but I'm worn-out." His gaze focused on the rolling fields outside the big picture window. "I've got to admit I'm surprised you're up and moving. Figured after last night you'd have packed your bags and be headed to your life in the city fast as your borrowed boots would take you."

"The boots are actually my old ones." Eli shrugged. "They're a little tight, but they fit about as well as this life ever did."

Cade's gaze locked on him, detached curiosity swimming in his eyes. "You ever miss it?"

Eli slid low in the recliner and crossed his hands loosely over his stomach. He took a second to figure out how to answer honestly. He'd realized in the past thirty-plus hours that there *were* things he missed.

Enough to come home?

Never.

His brother started to get up, shaking his head. "Your silence says more than enough."

"Sit," Eli ordered.

Cade's gaze narrowed.

"Please," he amended, breathing easier when Cade sank back onto the sofa. "It's just something I didn't expect you to ask, and I wanted to think about how best

to answer. If you'd asked me yesterday, I would've said
there was nothing I missed. Now?" He sat forward,
propping his forearms on his knees. "Yeah. There are
things I miss. Some more than others."

"Saw you with Reagan."

Eli's chin whipped up and his eyes locked on Cade's.
"I would argue there wasn't much to see."

"Depends on how hard someone was looking, I suppose." Crossing his arms over his chest, Cade considered Eli. "You came home for Ty."

The rest of the statement was left off but might as
well have been shouted—*but not for me.*

"Ty asked me to come home and help with the estate." Eli swallowed, weighing every word twice before
he continued. "You asked me to come home and stay.
I couldn't, Cade. I don't belong here."

"Did you ever consider that the two of us, me and Ty,
might have had dreams of our own? Your leaving meant
we were obligated to stay. Me particularly, because I
inherited the title of oldest whether I wanted it or not."

Resentment colored his every word, but the exhaus-
tion behind it all was what hit Eli the hardest. "I thought
you wanted to be here."

"What I wanted didn't matter after you took off.
Dad took me aside and explained what he expected.
You know how he was." Cade's gaze drifted back to
the window. "I didn't want to leave him, didn't want to
put it all on Ty." He faced Eli. "So I stayed."

"What did you want to do instead?" Eli asked quietly.

"Doesn't matter anymore." Standing, Cade stretched.
"I've got a conference call tomorrow at nine with a
difficult client. Dad's office have internet?"

"Dial-up. Doubt it's fast enough for what you need.

Reagan's place has satellite internet. We've used it before to place large orders."

"I'll ask her if I can use it, then. Thanks."

"No problem." Cade slapped his cowboy hat on. "State vet will be here at noon tomorrow. Wouldn't hurt to have you around to speak legalese."

"I'll be here."

"We'll see," Cade muttered, heading outside.

"Cade?" Eli called.

The man paused and glanced over his shoulder, one hand on the screen door, waiting.

"I won't leave you guys to handle this alone." It wasn't the apology Eli had intended to offer, but it was what came out. It was a place to start.

Cade gave a short nod and went on outside.

Eli pushed out of the chair and, without thinking too hard, grabbed the keys to one of the ranch trucks and headed out.

THE KNOCK AT the door dragged Reagan out of a deep sleep. Squinting at the late-afternoon sunlight, she sat up and rubbed her bleary eyes. Brisket had crashed out on his dog bed on the floor beside her, but the knock had brought the dog up on all fours facing the front of the house.

A toss of the quilt exposed her overheated skin to the air-conditioned room and goose bumps broke out all over. That's when she realized her hair was half-wrapped in the towel, the bottom half of its length still damp.

"Great," she muttered to the dog. "I'm going to open the door looking like Medusa. If I turn anyone to stone, you'll dig the hole to bury the evidence. Deal?"

He wagged his tail.

"Excellent." Shoving her feet into slippers, she finger combed her hair as best she could and started for the door.

A second, louder knock sounded.

"Coming!" Yes, she worked for people, but damn if their general impatience didn't make her a little crazy at times. She yanked the door open and nearly knocked herself over. "Eli?"

"Hey." His heated gaze roamed over her body, taking in her thin cami and tiny sleep shorts, before trailing down her legs and back up to her face. "Can I come in for a second?"

"Stay," she ordered Brisket. Heart pounding in her ears, she stepped out on the porch and pulled the door closed behind her. "I'm not sure it's the best idea right now."

He gave a short nod. "You're beautiful."

Heat burned her cheeks. "What are you doing here?"

"I have to talk to you."

Reagan's stomach plummeted. A hundred possible reasons why he would have come raced through her mind, but only one stuck. He was done with her. It had taken him one literal roll in the hay, and he was finished. "So talk."

Dark brows winged down over blue eyes. "You have a problem with letting me in your house for this conversation?"

"Some conversations don't need coffee and a couch. Just get it over with."

He jerked as if she'd slapped him. "This is quite a bit different than my reception this morning."

Lips thin, she lifted one shoulder in an approximation of a shrug.

Eli rolled his head. "I'm here to ask a favor."

That threw her. "I'm sorry?"

"A favor." Eli propped one hip on the porch rail. "I'd appreciate it if I could borrow your office tomorrow morning a little before nine. I have a conference call with a difficult client and some of my office staff. The ranch office doesn't have enough bandwidth to carry the call. Cade suggested I ask if I could use your place."

"You're here to borrow my office?" Heat crawled up her neck and across her cheeks.

"Yeah. Why? What did you think...?" His brows shot up. "You thought I was here to end this thing between us?"

She crossed her arms under her breasts and forced herself to meet his wide-eyed stare. "It crossed my mind."

Slowly standing, he moved toward her. The wild heat in his gaze said she couldn't have been any more wrong.

Reagan retreated up until she was pressed against the front door, her hand fumbling to find the doorknob. He reached out and gently grasped her wrist, pulling it forward and placing it around his neck. He did the same with her other hand. Then he bent, hooked his arms under her butt and lifted her straight up. "Legs around my waist."

"We're on my front porch," she whispered.

"In the middle of nowhere."

"Clients regularly come by without an appointment."

"Legs, Reagan."

She secretly reveled in his brute strength as she wrapped her legs around his waist. And gasped. The hard ridge of his erection rubbed at her sex through the seriously thin cotton of her sleep shorts. Her nipples beaded. Breaths came shallow and fast as he shifted her so her feminine lips parted. The rough edge of his jeans scraped tender flesh and she tightened her arms and legs around him. "Eli," she whispered roughly.

He supported her ass, fumbling to get his zipper down. The heat of his erection nearly scalded her skin as the broad head of his cock slipped inside her shorts. On contact, he buried his face in her neck and let out a tortured groan. "Damn it, Reagan. You're not wearing underwear."

"I got out of the shower and grabbed a nap."

"And now I'm not only thinking about you naked, but soapy and wet, too." He lifted his face and shared a tight smile with her. "You're trying to reduce me to the green kid I used to be and make me come before I've had my way with you." He dug his wallet out one-handed. "Condom's behind the driver's license."

Shoulders propped against the front door as he held her up by the thighs, she fumbled through his wallet, found the condom and tossed the wallet aside. He ripped the condom wrapper with his teeth and sheathed his erection. Then he was there, pushing inside her, giving no quarter as he pulled her down his length.

Chest to chest, he never took his eyes off hers. "You're so damn tight."

Gripping his hips and using his neck as a fulcrum, she pressed her forehead to his before she lifted herself up his length.

He hissed. "Sweet hell."

His mouth claimed hers with authority, challenging her to meet the thrust of his tongue in time with the thrust of his hips. The width of his cock stretched her to a point where pain and pleasure converged and she reveled in it. Every thrust was a kind of claiming. And the words he whispered in her ear, the things he said he was going to do to her, took her higher.

She rode him harder, leaning back far enough to force him to widen his stance and bend his knees a little more. Her tempo increased, nails digging into the soft skin on his neck. "Eli," she breathed, unable to stop herself from calling out his name.

Hands on her hips, he encouraged her to move faster, rougher. He leaned her forward just enough to ensure the root of his cock scraped her clit with every thrust.

Her eyes widened and, before she could think about how good that really felt, the orgasm crashed over her. Her walls tightened around him and her whole body shook with the ferocity of her release. She was carried away on a surge of pleasure unlike any she'd ever experienced.

His fingers dug into her ass and then, with a shout, he let go. Hips pumping hard, she felt the pulses along the length of his cock as his release moved through him. His movements became sporadic, slowed and then stopped. He pressed her shoulders against the front door, pinning her there with his chest as his hands gripped her thighs. Breathing raggedly, he laid a gentle kiss on her lips. "So, can I use your internet?"

The question was so off-the-wall that she burst out laughing. "For this? You can even use my long-distance service if the connection cuts out. Just don't touch my red Swingline stapler."

He narrowed his eyes as he set her down. "What would I have to do to be able to use the stapler?"

"I'm not sure you're cut out for it," she said, getting her feet under her.

Turning, she opened the door and Brisket jumped out, tail wagging. He went straight to Eli and pressed his body up against the man's leg. Big brown eyes lifted to watch as Eli tucked himself inside his jeans and zipped up.

The ease with which Brisket accepted Eli made her

chest tight. It was as if the man just belonged, and that was the farthest thing from the truth that could possibly be said. From his expensive haircut to his smooth hands with their fresh blisters, Eli didn't belong here. Never had. This could only last a few days at most, and then he'd be gone. They'd both be in the places they belonged, both alone again, though he was certain not to stay that way, whereas she seemed tormented by ghosts.

"Hey, buddy." Eli rubbed the dog's ears. "Let's get inside." He gestured awkwardly to his groin. "I would pay good money to have the chance to clean up." Brisket trotted into the house. "Smart dog," Eli commented.

"Brilliant," she answered, watching the dog curiously. Trying to recapture the lighthearted mood of moments before, she looked over her shoulder as she headed inside. "Seems his judge of character might be warped, but he's hell on cattle so I'll keep him."

"Hey!" Eli slapped her ass. "My character's just fine."

"Your character's as warped as an untreated two-by-four left out through a good wet season."

"Wench," he growled, scooping her up and starting for the bathroom.

Panic struck her as unexpectedly as a rattlesnake strike. "No. Don't go into the bathroom. I don't want to use the bathroom."

Eli stopped and glanced down at her, the deep V between his brows seeming unnatural. "I'm seriously hoping you're not suggesting we use the stock tanks. Always makes me nervous to dunk my junk in there. A lot of those tanks have catfish." He shuddered.

"Put me down. Please."

He set her on her feet. "What's wrong?"

She pushed her hair off her forehead. How did she

explain that this entire house was tied to Luke? How did she tell Eli that she couldn't do this here, have him in the space that Luke had loved so dearly? The porch had pushed boundaries. This blew past them without slowing down to even appreciate the posted emotional speed limit.

"Reagan?"

Truth, then. "This is Luke's house."

Eli studied her until she couldn't meet his direct stare any longer.

His boot steps advertised his approach. Prepared for his touch, she didn't flinch when he gently grasped her chin and encouraged her to meet his eyes. "I respect the fact this was your late husband's house. Would you prefer I use the guest bath?"

She opened and closed her mouth. Words eluded her.

"Which way?" he asked, scanning the open living room.

"Second door on the left," Reagan croaked, pointing in the opposite direction.

"Catch you out here in fifteen? I'd like to shower really fast."

"You're not mad?" she whispered.

His lips were soft, the kiss tender. "Never."

She watched him stride down the hall in the direction she'd indicated and stood there until the door to the spare bath clicked closed.

Moving like an automaton, she turned toward her bedroom. Five minutes to clean up and dress. She couldn't let herself think about anything else, couldn't let history catch up to her. Because if she stood still too long, it wouldn't just catch up with her, it would level her.

That was the power of ghosts.

11

Eli made himself at home while he waited for Reagan to emerge, grabbing a beer from the fridge and sinking into the deep sofa. Guilt that he hadn't thought this through very well—being in her private space with Luke—rankled. Somehow, he needed to make it up to her. He didn't know how, wasn't sure what to do to show her he respected where she was coming from, but he'd figure it out. She deserved nothing less.

There was a sharp knock on the door and he twisted to look out the front windows. A brown Ford four-by-four hauling a four-horse pipe trailer had pulled up with an enormous Charolais bull throwing enough of a fit that the parked truck was being pushed around like a Tonka toy. A second knock sounded but, this time, the door opened a crack.

"Doc Matthews?" a man called out.

"Coming," she shouted. Hair pulled back in a French braid, she came out of the bedroom with her boots in hand. She paused, glancing between Eli and the fifty-ish man standing in the doorway. "Hey, Gary. What's going on?"

The man's identity clicked with Eli. Gary Watson

had been a good friend of his father's, regularly stopping by to shoot the breeze. Growing up, Eli had done some day work on the Watson ranch off and on, though he'd never cared for the Watson family much. Gary's wife, Linda, always had her nose in business that had nothing to do with her. And she had a gift for pulling other noses in alongside hers. She might not be well respected, but when you wanted to know something, the Watson number was the first one you called.

Gary looked between Reagan, freshly showered, and Eli, also freshly showered, and the older man's eyes visibly cooled. "Found a wallet on your porch, Doc." He tossed it on the nearest counter.

"That'd be mine," Eli said. "Must've dropped it when I stopped in to ask Doc Matthews if I could borrow her internet service. Thanks for picking it up." Eli stood and moved to place himself between Reagan and Watson's assessing stare. "How've you been?"

"Heard you'd come back to handle the estate," Watson said .

He struggled to keep his free hand loose instead of letting it fist as he wanted to. "I did, yes."

"Rumor has it your old man left a hell of a mess—a mess we might all end up paying for." Gary's voice was thick as he spoke around the dip tucked between his bottom lip and teeth. The words were soft, the allegation clear.

"Rumors are nasty business," Eli answered just as softly, picking up his wallet and tucking it into his back pocket. "They tend to be based on a lot of false assumptions that only end up fostering a lot of nonsense and hurting innocent people. Hate to think of such a tight community as this singling someone out without all their facts straight."

The other man's eyes narrowed. "You got something to say, boy?"

"I was Max Covington's boy. Not yours. And if I have something to say, I'll have the good grace to say it to your face." Eli took a long draw on his beer. "Never doubt it."

Reagan stepped around Eli and tipped her head toward the truck in her drive. "What've you got, Gary?"

"The wrong vet." Spinning on his heel, he yanked the front door closed behind him, his booted steps heavy on the stair treads as he stormed off the porch.

Eli rammed his beer bottle on the counter and took off after Gary. Hell, if the man hadn't lit his fuse with a damn blowtorch.

"Eli!"

"Stay inside, Reagan," he snapped, shutting the door before hopping off the porch and eating up the distance between him and the retreating man. "Hold it, Watson."

The man got in his truck and tried to slam the door, but Eli caught it and held it open. "You have a problem with me or my family? Fine. I've got no problem working it out with you with either civil words or fists. Your choice. But that's between us. You leave Reagan out of it. She works for our place just as she works for yours."

"She don't work for us no more." Watson spit a glob of tarry mess at Eli's boots. "I'd deal with the devil himself before I'd pay that woman another dime, doing Luke's memory wrong with the likes of you."

"Watch your mouth," Eli snarled, leaning into the truck and grabbing Gary by the front of the shirt. "She's a good woman."

"Oughta clean up after yourselves a little better if you're gonna be screwing around where God and country can see." Gary's smile was vicious. "Condom wrapper's tucked inside your wallet. Safe sex don't make her any less a—"

Eli threw up his arm to level the man, but Reagan grabbed him. He hadn't even heard her come up behind him. She shoved him back a step and put herself between the two men. Skin pale, her eyes were livid pools of green fire. "Don't you *dare* come onto my property and accuse me of disrespecting my late husband's memory. He's been gone for three years, and I've done nothing but honor him day in and day out."

"You deny you screwed a Covington?" Gary demanded.

"I don't owe you any answers."

"And that's answer enough," the man said on a sneer. "Luke's probably rolling in his grave."

All the color left her face so fast Eli thought she might faint. He should have known she was made of tougher stuff than that.

Her fist connected with Watson's mouth in a short, sharp jab that bloodied both his upper and lower lips. "Use my phone if you want to call in the assault, you son of a bitch, but don't you ever, *ever* insult Luke in front of me again. Now get the hell off my land. I don't care if your cows come down with chlamydia and your whole herd aborts. Don't call me for help."

Slamming his door, she spun away from the truck and stalked to the house, calling over her shoulder, "Come in or don't, Eli. Your choice."

He couldn't help it. With a parting smile at Gary Watson and his stunned, bleeding face, Eli turned and sauntered up the steps, across the porch and into the house. He shut the door behind him with authority and locked the door.

Continuing across the room, he came up behind Reagan, spun her around to face him and kissed the hell out of her. When he finally came up for air, he was grinning. "That was the sexiest thing *ever*. I'm talking in the history of man, darlin'."

"I think I broke a knuckle."

Glancing at her swelling hand, he leaned down and placed his lips on the split skin with extreme care. "Let's get some ice on that."

"Eli?"

He glanced up.

"Thanks for taking up for me."

He felt his face go slack. "Did you really think I'd do different? I mean, I understand you wanted me to keep it a secret and I agreed, but Reagan, he'd already figured it out. I wasn't about to let him disrespect you."

"I heard what he said—about finding the condom wrapper. He's going to gossip." She let out a shaky sigh. "Everyone is going to know."

He blinked slowly. "Know what, exactly?"

"About this." She waggled her good hand between them. "About us."

"Then I'm not hiding it." He held up a hand when she opened her mouth, presumably to argue. "Did Luke love you?"

"What?" she gasped.

"Did he love you?"

"Yes."

"Would he want you to be miserable?" She didn't answer immediately, so he pressed. "Well? Would he?"

"No," she whispered so softly he read her lips more than heard her speak.

"Then don't be miserable. If he loved you, he'd want you to be happy, and if what we've got makes you happy—" he cupped her face in his hands "—run with it."

"The problem is that this is a fifty-yard dash," she said, "not a marathon. It'll be over and done, my business will be ruined and you'll be gone. Again."

If what he heard in her voice was true, it sounded as if she might regret his leaving. Eli's heart slammed against his sternum. Taking a deep breath, Eli pressed his forehead to hers and closed his eyes. "Let's take this one day at a time, okay? We'll figure it out as we go. But I want to be very clear on one thing."

She closed her eyes. "What?"

"Look at me." When she hesitated, he leaned away just enough to give her a very gentle shake. "Look at me, Reagan."

Her eyes slowly opened.

"Whatever happens between us? It's between *us*. Understand? We don't owe anyone any explanation, nor do we owe anyone an apology. Your work speaks for itself, and I doubt anyone with sense will take their business elsewhere."

Her nod was all he got out of her in the way of agreement, but it would have to do. Because now that this thing between him and Reagan was about to become public knowledge, the opportunity to turn this into a marathon became very real.

He just had to figure out how fast to set the initial pace.

Eli LEFT NOT long after binding her hand in an ice pack. She hadn't wanted to be alone, but at the same time, after the incident with Gary Watson, she hadn't wanted Eli to stay.

The older man's vitriolic verbal attack had left her more shaken than she cared to admit. No doubt his wife would fire up the gossip train the moment Gary got home, burning up the phone lines with the news about the condom wrapper and wallet on the porch. The woman would back up her circumstantial evidence with the image of Eli relaxing in her house as Reagan came out of the bedroom barefoot and with wet hair. As the gossip was retold, the story would be sensationalized until she was wearing a dominatrix getup and Eli had on little more than a pony saddle cinched tight to his back. The idea alone made her grin.

Then she sobered. Lord, this was going to be such a mess. Three years of fighting to be the proper widow and maintain a reputation as an ethical businessperson and she'd blown it with one spontaneous act carried out with the county's very own black sheep.

Now, lying in bed and wide-awake a little after five in the morning, she had little choice but to get up and get the day started. The state vet would be at the Covington ranch by noon, and the guy was thorough.

She had ordered extra vaccine, and she'd be working all morning to continue treating the infected cattle, isolating the sickest, euthanizing those beyond hope and centrally pasturing those who should make it after they'd been dosed. The entire thing would be a circus where she was the ringmaster and every hoop she had to jump through blazed.

Brisket whined in his sleep, and she automatically dropped a foot to his bed and rubbed his back. He snorted and sat up, stretching.

"Morning, sunshine." In a moment of indulgence, she patted the bed and encouraged him up to cuddle with her. The dog snuggled into her side and sighed, totally content.

Reagan couldn't help but wonder what life would have been like if she'd taken Ty up on his offer not to be their vet. None of this would have happened; she wouldn't be faced with attitudes like Gary Watson's, and she would be…what? Hiding out at home trying to avoid Eli?

Shame nearly choked her. She was a bigger person than that. Never had she expected she'd allow history to dictate both her present and her future.

But that's exactly what you've been doing, her conscience whispered.

The thought stilled her hand on her dog's fur. She'd been a coward. It had begun the moment Eli walked away from her that summer night. Ever since then, she'd clung to what might have been and had missed everything that might be. She had to get out of the house. Get out of the immediate reach of Luke's clothes that she hadn't gotten rid of, their wedding pictures, the furniture he'd picked out to surprise her. The stupid antelope head he'd hung on the living room wall.

This place was so much his, so much *him*, and always had been. She'd never considered what it did to her to come home to this every day, to live surrounded by the memories he'd worked so hard to create.

"No more," she whispered. Change was inevitable. It would have been the same whether he'd lived or died. And if he'd lived and Eli had come home?

She jumped from the bed and pulled on the first clothes she found. Whatever might have been, it was just that: might have been. Luke was gone. She'd been living in the shadow of his death for three years, burdened by her guilt, burdened by the community's expectations, burdened by what she'd always wanted versus her reality. Never had she been so ashamed.

She'd been living life like a spectator with a crappy view from the cheap seats. She'd allowed the blind expectations of others to dictate her behavior. She'd spent a sleepless night worrying about the likes of the Watsons. She was done with that.

She wasn't going to spend the rest of her life living on the fringes. If Eli's return had shown her anything, it was that she had more left in her—more life, desire, determination, pride—than she'd given herself credit for.

And if Eli is wrong? If the community continues to rally around Luke's memory and you lose everything? her conscience pressed.

"I'm stronger than a bunch of wagging tongues," she said aloud. "I'll manage." No, that wasn't true. She wouldn't just manage. She was going to come out on top of this mess and reclaim a life she'd been too scared to live. And if people didn't like it?

She'd heard Hell had a handful of openings, and she'd be happy to provide personal recommendations to the devil himself.

12

ELI KNOCKED A second time on Reagan's front door, but no one answered. A glance at his watch told him he had ten minutes to get into her office and log on or his meeting was going to go ass up. No help for it. He'd have to break in.

A sprint to the barn provided a shovel. Even though it was necessary, he still felt bad smashing a windowpane on her front door. Of course he'd replace it, but it wouldn't have come to this if she'd just stayed to let him in. Or left the key under a flowerpot. Or something. Anything.

A quick circuit of the house revealed her office. It looked entirely different than the rest of the house, more feminine in a wild way, less manly hunter/rancher somehow.

He signed into his computer and growled when the internet turned out to be password protected. Grabbing her phone, he called Cade. His brother answered on the second ring, and Eli didn't give him a chance to get through his hello before he asked, "What's the password to Reagan's Wi-Fi?"

"Hold on. I should remember this."

Eli listened to Cade breathing, his own anxiety mounting with his brother's every breath. "I've got to be online in—" another peek at his watch "—two minutes."

"Try *RedCanoe#2*," he said, spelling it out.

Eli's fingers fumbled over the keyboard. "Come again?"

"RedCanoe#2," Cade repeated. "Why? It mean something?"

"It's nothing. Thanks for this. I'll be there before the state guy." Hanging up, he typed the password in and the Wi-Fi began the process of connecting.

"RedCanoe#2." He shook his head, a small smile playing at his lips. They'd lied to their parents one weekend and snuck away together, going up to the Abiquiu Reservoir and camping out in the back of his pickup. They'd rented a canoe, the red one numbered *two*, and fished and laughed and found a remote area to beach the little boat and make love on a blanket on the sand. The sun had been hot on their skin. She'd ridden him, a dark outline in the bright light, her hair blowing in the breeze. He'd realized then that he'd never love anyone else the way he loved her. He'd told her so.

And she remembered.

Throat tight, he plugged his earpiece in and signed into Skype. His screen immediately flashed an incoming call. Taking a deep breath, he cleared his throat and answered. "Elijah Covington."

"Mr. Covington, Ms. English and I are present. I've not been able to reach Mr. Macallroy yet."

"Give him five minutes. If he's not here, we'll call his secretary," Eli responded absently, scrolling through the settlement offer on-screen and his handwritten notes in the small file he'd brought with him.

"How are things, Eli?" Amanda asked.

"My brothers and I are doing what we can…" He trailed off, realizing his mistake.

"You have brothers?" the other attorney asked. "I had no idea."

"I prefer to keep my personal and professional lives separate." He fought to keep his voice calm and cool. "The two don't intersect for me. Ever."

"Fair enough." Papers rustled in the background. "What's the point of today's call? Macallroy Oil is getting off with a proverbial slap on the wrist with this EPA fine. Does the word *Valdez* not mean anything to him?"

"He believes we're not representing him vigorously enough in seeking a smaller fine." Eli continued to flip through his notes. "Feels the environmental impact isn't equivalent to some of the larger oil spills we've seen previously."

"Another case of size mattering," Amanda muttered.

Lynette coughed to cover her laugh.

"Try him again, Lynette," Eli said, ignoring the by-play.

"Don Macallroy's office," his secretary answered.

It was right then that Eli officially despised Macallroy. They'd rung his personal computer, and he'd set it up so his secretary had answered. Such a bullshit power play. Fighting to keep his cool, Eli pulled his professionalism around him like a chain mail cloak. "Good morning, Susan. Will you please let Mr. Macallroy know that his legal team is present and available for the call?"

"Certainly, Mr. Covington. Please hold."

Seconds later, Don came online. "Covington," he said in greeting. "Mike Tibbs, Jeff Orr and Ron Tucker are sitting in." In the background, computer keys clicked.

Eli did his best to ignore the fact Macallroy had es-

sentially dismissed the women on the call by refusing
to acknowledge them. It wasn't a secret that the guy
was a dick. Still, it ate at Eli. He opened his mouth to
say something, but Amanda stepped in.

"Good morning, Don." Her chilled voice conveyed
her displeasure.

"English," Don replied.

"I understand you're unhappy with the EPA's settlement figures," she continued.

"Eli and I have already talked. No need to rehash
the fact your firm dropped the ball on this one." The
old man's gaze bored into the laptop camera. "So, Eli,
what are you going to do about it?"

"Nothing." It was out before Eli could temper his
response.

"Excuse me?" Don's voice was lethally quiet. "For a
moment there, I thought you said 'nothing.'"

Eli parked his elbows on the desk and steepled his
fingers in front of him, forefingers tapping against each
other. "The EPA has every right to seek three times this
amount in damages. They've agreed to settle based on
a hell of a lot of negotiating we've done on Macallroy
Oil's behalf. Meanwhile, your company is going to be
tied up in a public relations nightmare for years. You'd
be better off to spend the money the EPA isn't demanding investing in an aggressive, environmentally friendly
PR campaign to win back the public's good opinion.
Show you give a damn about the impact the oil spill is
going to have over the coming years."

Don stared at him, unblinking. "I think we're done
here, gentlemen. You and I will sit down, face-to-face,
and work this out, Covington. Your grief has clearly
screwed up your perspective. I'm willing to discount
that. Once. Get your ass back to Austin by the middle

of next week or Macallroy Oil will find alternate representation from this point forward."

The screen went blank.

Eli closed his eyes and did his best to avoid the nausea swamping his gut. "Amanda, Lynette, I've got to be somewhere in the next hour so there's not time to discuss this. Lynette, make arrangements for me to meet Don at Peché next Thursday evening for drinks and dinner. And get me a new iPhone overnighted." He rattled off the ranch's address as he shoved paperwork into his briefcase.

He wasn't delusional. The founding partners would have his ass if Macallroy fired the firm. The account was one of the most lucrative year after year, and being awarded the account had been a major coup when he'd made senior partner.

Don had always rubbed him the wrong way. But this was the first time Eli had allowed it to show. He needed to return to Austin and get his game back. This whole experience, being at the ranch, reconnecting with his brothers, being with Reagan—it was throwing him off. Badly.

But he wasn't ready to leave Reagan. She'd weighed on his mind all night and throughout the morning. They'd rediscovered something in each other, a once-in-a-lifetime passion. If they stood a chance of recapturing that passion, they had to get away from the stresses of the ranch quarantine. So why not invite her to come with him to Austin? What he could offer her now was exponentially more than the pipe dreams he'd laid at her feet as a teen. And it was so much more than she had here. Better yet, he could get her away from the gossip hounds that would be dogging her—*their*—heels before the day was out.

If he could get her to agree to go, even for a long weekend, he could show her around the city, romance her more than a little and open her eyes to the life they could share there. And if she felt even half as much for him now as she had all those years ago, they had a real opportunity of making something of this unexpected second chance.

Only yesterday he'd thought his biggest challenge would be figuring out how to convince her they could run the race together. But sitting in her office, considering what it would take to persuade her to come to Austin, he knew he'd been wrong.

His biggest challenge was going to be getting her to agree to leave everything she knew behind.

"WE'RE DOING ALL we can, Dr. Alvarez."

Reagan listened as Cade spoke with the New Mexico state vet. He'd shown up almost two hours early. To say he hadn't been thrilled with what he'd found would be an understatement. Granted, he'd had nothing but praise for Reagan's diagnosis and treatment plan, but Cade had argued it was excessive and would put the ranch out of business.

Ty stood by, taking it all in. He refused to look at her, and that got under her skin.

She'd done what she had to do, not only ethically but legally, and the brothers were going to have to accept that. Yes, the treatment plan she'd come up with was pricey, but it was the only way she knew to contain the disease and keep it from spreading. Already three of the calves she'd held from the Jensen place had tested positive for the same disease. If it continued to spread, there would be little they could do but quarantine the county.

That would cut into profitability for all the ranches, and the Covingtons were sure to bear the blame.

"Armando?" Reagan said, addressing the state vet by first name as she stepped forward to break up what was fast becoming an argument.

He faced her, his irritation undisguised.

She held up her hands, palms out. "Let's take this down a notch. There are some options here, things we haven't touched on yet."

A truck roared up the dirt drive and slid to a stop in front of the nearest bunkhouse. Eli stepped out dressed in complete business attire.

Her heart flipped over. She might always think of—and prefer—him in his jeans and tees, but he was freaking *GQ* gorgeous all decked out like he was. The dark expression on his face didn't bode well, though. He looked like he wanted to kill someone with one hand while the other mixed up a strong drink as a chaser to the violence.

He walked up and held out a hand to the man wearing the state's insignia on his sleeve. "You must be Dr. Alvarez. I'm Elijah Covington. I'm representing the ranch in this investigation."

"Are you an attorney, Mr. Covington?" Armando asked.

"I am."

"Then I don't have much use for you." He held up a hand when Eli protested. "The law is the law in this instance, and you can file all the injunctions you want to stop me, but I'm the state-appointed expert. Dr. Matthews has done all the right things, suggested all the most effective treatments, but she also reported a second case involving three steers earlier this morning."

Eli turned his burning gaze on her. "She did?"

"She's ethically obligated to report these things when there's a threat of outbreak." Armando shifted, but Eli didn't look away from Reagan.

His fury was undisguised, as if she'd betrayed him. Then she remembered he'd needed to use her office this morning. She winced. He only arched a brow and faced Armando.

The vet crossed his arms over his chest. "Do you have an insurance policy for the cattle you've contracted to feed out?"

Reagan's stomach fell. "Armando, I don't think we've got to talk about euthanizing in large numbers. Not yet."

He gazed at her, eyes flat but knowing. "It's spreading, Reagan. Until my team and I identify the source, we've got to keep this ranch quarantined and the sickest of the cattle have to be killed off. If we don't, we're just perpetuating the disease and delaying recovery in those that stand even half a chance of making it."

"So that's what your criteria are?" Eli demanded. "We kill everything with less than a fifty-percent chance of survival?" Cade laid a hand on his shoulder, but Eli shrugged it off. "An answer, please, Dr. Alvarez."

"Frankly? Yes."

"You'll ruin the Covington ranch," Eli all but snarled. "I won't allow you to do that." Shoulders tight and neck corded with fury, he rounded on Reagan. "This ranch is my brothers' livelihood. You can't take that from them."

Ty stepped forward and laid a hand on his oldest brother's arm. "Eli—"

Armando interrupted. "I'll say it again—there's nothing you can do to stop me. I have a duty to the State of New Mexico and the states that border her to keep the cattle population healthy. Bovine Respiratory

Disease has one of the highest fatality rates of all the cattle diseases. We'll kill off those Dr. Matthews and I deem to have less than a fifty percent chance and burn the carcasses. I'll make arrangement with the Bureau of Land Management to set up a burn zone. The ranch will be financially responsible for funding the firefighters necessary, as well as the equipment they'll have to bring in."

Reagan's heart skipped several beats and then took up a thundering pace when she realized the role she was going to have to play in assessing the herds. She would probably shutter the Bar C. She gripped her shirt at the waist and wadded the fabric, doing her best to keep from shaking. The Covington brothers would never forgive her for this.

Eli stepped up close to Armando, eyes blazing. "I'll make this clear. Once. I don't care what it costs, but you and Dr. Matthews *will* resolve this issue as expeditiously as possible with the end goal of lifting the quarantine on the ranch so these calves can be fed out and shipped before the end of this year."

Cade's voice was tight when he tried to interrupt. "We can't afford—"

"The hell with the costs, Cade." When Cade opened his mouth, presumably to argue, Eli's mouth thinned and his eyes narrowed as he looked first at Cade and then at Ty. "Not a damn word from either of you. This ranch is your legacy. It will *not* be shut down by some self-righteous prick who thinks that because he's been issued a plastic badge and a cheap flip wallet with a state ID, he can come out here and drop a can of whoop-ass, forcing us to run for cover."

"It's the actual costs, Eli," Ty said quietly.

"I'll cover the costs. You're my brothers, and I'd move heaven and hell to see you done right by."

"Between treatment and the burn zone, you're looking at roughly $70,000, Mr. Covington."

Reagan wanted to tell Armando to shut the hell up, to not press Eli when he was so close to losing his temper. The words would have been wasted, though.

Eli rounded on the state vet. "Your personal concern for my financial solvency is touching, Doctor," Eli said, the sound of his voice as soft as a large blade slicing through the air. "Allow me to alleviate your concern that you might not get paid. I'll have my bank wire the initial estimate plus an additional thirty per cent for unforeseen expenses and any overages we may encounter. The funds will be in the Bar C's primary account within seventy-two hours per regulations established by the Federal Reserve. If that timeline isn't good enough for you, take it up with their local office. The money *will* be there. So, by all means, don't let the financial details get in the way of your intent to slaughter and burn the sick and infirm."

Armando shifted to face Reagan, effectively dismissing Eli. "We'll use established criteria to determine which animals are treated and which are euthanized."

She nodded numbly. "Give me a minute, Armando."

He tipped his chin in acknowledgment and started for his truck.

"What happens now?" Ty asked quietly.

"We'll set up a working pen in the first pasture away from the house. All the animals will be run through and assessed." She swallowed hard. "Those that aren't deemed candidates for survival will be put down. It'll be over in about three days, and in another ten days, we can begin the process of applying to the state to lift the quarantine. We just have to prove recovery and clean stock tanks, burn off any residual hay the sick cattle may have encountered, scrape the corrals clean..." She laid a hand on Eli's arm. "We'll work through this."

Eli jerked away from her. "If we treated humans like this, 'euthanizing' those we weren't sure we could save, we'd be labeled sadistic bastards at best, radical supremacists at worst. And there's little difference between the two." Grabbing his briefcase off the ground, he started for the house.

She made to follow him, but Cade moved into her path. "Give him a little while. Killing was always hard on him."

"He doesn't have to do it," she objected.

"Yeah, he does. Don't forget who he is. He won't ask someone to do his dirty work just to cut himself an easy path. We have Dad to thank for that. He forced Eli to put down his first horse when it developed hoof problems. The animal could have been saved, but Dad said it would be cheaper to invest in a new horse and he didn't need a cripple running around. Made Eli pull the trigger. He always had Eli do the worst work. Claimed he was trying to toughen him up."

She swallowed hard. "How old was he?"

"When he had to shoot his horse?" Cade shook his head. "Probably seven. Maybe eight."

Her stomach protested, forcing her to swallow convulsively.

Cade looked at Eli's retreating back. "Never got used to that part of ranch life. Running like he did was the only way he could get out of that cycle. I didn't really understand that until I watched him work side by side with us the other night, hanging in with the tasks I was sure would be hardest for him. Caught him puking behind the barn after he shot the first steer. It might have taken me years to realize getting out was his best option, but it doesn't make it any less true."

"But—"

"Leave it alone, okay?" Cade followed after Eli, who'd slammed into the house. "Call it whatever lets you sleep at night, Reagan. What we're being asked to do is killing in more ways than one."

Cade meant this could be the death of the ranch itself. She knew it, but she couldn't think about that. Not right now. First she had to stop this from spreading and save the animals she could save.

Then she'd deal with the heartache eating a hole in her chest, the one that said by doing the right thing, she just might lose Eli all over again.

13

THE NEXT FEW days were hell. Between attending the probate hearing, confirming his dad had less than $20,000 in cash assets and working through the stocker herds one animal at a time, Eli managed very little sleep. He spent his waking hours split between wearing loafers and cowboy boots, business suits and shit-stained jeans. Never had he been pulled in such opposite directions.

His new cell arrived, and immediately the firm's founding partners began calling. The first two days they were cajoling, joking with him about getting back to civilization. By Monday, their coaxing turned to demands he return. He had, after all, taken his three days of bereavement leave. They needed him to be in the office to handle Macallroy, who was making serious noises about taking his business elsewhere. And, to add to the soup pot of madness, Lynette had begun to call three or four times a day to ask for guidance.

Before the last call, he'd just pulled the trigger to put a young steer down. His stomach had been rolling viciously, and he seriously thought he might lose his lunch.

"What?" he'd shouted into the phone.

"M-Mr. Covington?"

"Not now, Lynette. Go find Amanda if you have questions." And he'd hung up.

They'd sorted the sickest first and, so far, they'd put down more than forty percent of the herds that had moved through the portable corrals. It seemed the rest stood a fairly good chance of making it, but it would mean more round-the-clock work, and he had just about reached his limit.

He and Reagan hadn't exchanged much more than curt conversation as they worked together. Often when he'd grab a couple hours of sleep, he'd wake to find her still at it. She had to be near breaking, too. He'd been so angry with her for all of this, but it wasn't her fault. Realization had taken a few days to set in, but when it did, it had been one more brick of guilt to weigh him down. She hadn't brought this down on them. Not in any way. All she'd done was her job. She'd held to her ethics and obligations, and that was more than he could say for himself lately.

Still, ethics aside, this whole experience had reinforced his long-held belief that this wasn't the life for him. Facing life and death every day, never knowing if you'd be delivering a calf or putting its mother down after a difficult birth—he couldn't live this way. Ranching life was far too brutal. He wanted to give life every chance to persevere. That's why he'd gone into law, though he'd lost some of that idealism along the way.

He had to wrap this up and get home…to Austin, back to a job he was damned good at with people he didn't have to share a house with or a lover he couldn't touch. But he wouldn't abandon his brothers again. He might not be a cowboy, but there were other ways he could help them and the legacy the three of them shared as brothers. He emptied the chamber of his rifle and bowed his head. The urge to plead with the heavens hit him for the second time since he'd started this journey, surprising him no less now than it had when the plane had dropped to the runway.

That's when it hit him—it was far too quiet. Dragging his gaze up, he looked around stupidly. *Where were all the cows?*

A hand settled on his shoulder and he glanced up.

"It's done," Ty said quietly.

"Finished?"

"In more ways than one." Cade handed him a sheet of paper. "The insurance company's dropping us. We won't be able to register or advertise as an insured stocker operation anymore." He swallowed hard and tipped his chin back, but not before Eli caught the sheen in his eyes. "The Bar C is done."

"No." Eli's denial surprised them all. Ty's gaze slowly rose even as Cade wiped his eyes without shame. "It's not done," Eli said vehemently. "This isn't how this was supposed to go."

Cade opened his mouth and had to close it as the first tear tipped over his lower lashes. He spun away and started across the pasture, away from the house and the day's activities.

They watched him go, and Eli experienced the strongest sense of solidarity with his brothers he'd ever had. He looked at Ty. "There has to be something we can do, something to change the course we're on."

Ty's usual fun-loving gaze was flat. "We ought to be able to make enough off the sale to buy a small place somewhere, but it won't be enough to use as a sole source of income. We'll have to take jobs with some of the local contractors around." He blew out a hard breath.

"Or sell, save the money and see if we can get hired on as cowboys on other ranches."

"No," Eli ground out, low but fierce. "I have a substantial savings account. I'll buy into the ranch, fund what I can and get a loan for the rest of it to restock the place. We'll just become an independent operation."

Ty gaped at him, face entirely blank. "We?"

Eli opened and closed his mouth. Then the laughter started, soft at first until it had him doubled over. "I've lost my damn mind," he finally said as he stood, "but yeah—*we*."

"You coming home?" Ty asked so quietly Eli had to ask him to repeat it. "Are you coming home, to the ranch?"

"No. I'll keep my job in Austin to insure this place stays afloat. Besides, if any of us should work in town, it's me. I'm better at it, and I make damn good money." Ty's face lost the joy that had suffused it, and Eli reached out to clasp his brother's shoulder. "It's for the best. I'll funnel everything I can back to you guys, and make some investments so we've got money for the lean years. It'll give you and Cade the security you have to have in order to make the Bar C what it should be without depending on brokers. I…" He rubbed a hand across of the nape of his neck and stared at his boots. "The Bar C has to stay in the family, if for no other reason than for you and the family of your own that you'll have one day. You *and* Cade, provided there's a woman out there tough enough to whip him into shape and keep him there. It won't happen for me, but I can make that happen for you two. I want to do that. Please."

Ty nodded and then started across the pasture in a different direction than Cade had taken, his shoulders shaking and head bowed.

Eli hurt for his brothers. They'd borne so much on their own, carrying his weight, his obligations, his legacy for him while he tried to find out who he was and where he belonged. The least he could do was ensure they both had the opportunity to make something of this place. Cade was a good businessman. Ty was an amazing horseman. Both were outstanding cowboys. Between them and the men they had on staff, they could make this work. He'd be a silent partner, and he wouldn't regret it in any way.

Grabbing his rifle, he headed toward the corrals. Several of the Bar C cowboys spoke to him, their deference clear. He'd held with them, worked alongside them and he'd earned their respect. It wasn't something he'd expected. It also wasn't something he'd ever take for granted. Eli searched for Reagan but couldn't find her anywhere. The state vet, though, was sitting in his truck, driver's door open, and filling out paperwork on a metal clipboard. Eli approached the man with caution. They hadn't gotten off on the right foot, and Eli had some fences to mend. The other man had to be receptive, though.

"Dr. Alvarez?" Eli started.

The vet glanced up, his hooded eyes emotionless. "Mr. Covington. What can I do for you?"

Eli held out his hand.

Dr. Alvarez set his stuff down slowly, stood and shook the proffered hand. "Different kind of discussion than I expected."

"I want to apologize for being so harsh the other day." A good eight inches taller than the diminutive man, Eli tried not to lord his height. "I was upset and struck out at the first target I could find."

Dr. Alvarez dropped Eli's hand and got back in his

truck, picking up his paperwork and returning his attention to it as he spoke. "I appreciate the apology, but I want to be clear that this won't change my recommendations for the ranch."

"I'm sorry?" Eli took his hat off and scrubbed a hand through his hair. "I was under the impression that we'd be cleared once the stock tanks were sanitized and the ear tags confirmed we'd accounted for all the calves."

The vet shot him a brief glance before continuing to fill out forms. "This is the worst outbreak I've seen in my career. It's spread to two additional ranches now. The Phillips just reported six head with symptoms. Until this is totally shut down, I'm quarantining the county."

"You—"

Dr. Alvarez held up a hand and gave Eli a somewhat compassionate look. "I realize what this is going to cost you. On the heels of losing your father, I would imagine it's harder than it would normally be. I'm sorry for that. But we can't jeopardize the state's cattle population on sentimentality, Mr. Covington."

"I understand," he said woodenly. Everything he'd just talked to his brothers about, everything he'd promised them he'd do, meant more now than ever. They'd have to begin an extensive recovery program and bring in cows as soon as the quarantine was lifted. To keep his word to his brothers, he'd have to sell his Lake Travis home, probably his car, and pare back his lifestyle by half. He'd do what he'd promised them he'd do, though.

His brothers would be able to live the life they'd fought so hard to hold on to. He wanted that for them, if not for himself.

Still, the achievement left him feeling empty. He'd

be returning to Austin with a true relationship with his brothers. But in the end? He'd still be going home just as alone as he had been when he arrived.

Unless he could convince Reagan to come with him...

REAGAN SAT ON the back porch of her house sipping beer and rocking her porch swing with one bare foot. The sunset blazed furiously as if the day protested the coming night. But like so many things in life, night would come no matter how hard the sun fought to hold its place.

Armando had left more than an hour ago with his final report. He'd told her he'd be quarantining the county, which meant more work for her. She couldn't bring herself to charge the ranchers for her services, not when the medications were so expensive, so she'd provide top-notch care at cut-rate prices until everyone was on their feet again. It was the right thing to do. But, like everything these days, it came with a cost.

Holding a hand up to shield her eyes, she watched her horses coming up to the barn for the night. Chores were done save stabling those four and feeding them. She'd get to it soon enough.

Brisket rolled over on his back, his tongue lolling out the side of his mouth. He swished his tail against the pine boards, and she gave in, rubbing his belly with her other foot. She absently reached for the phone and dialed her neighbor's number from memory.

Mark Russell picked up on the third ring. "Hey, Reagan. You okay?"

"I'm good, Mark. Have you heard otherwise?"

He chuckled. "The Watsons are burning up the phone lines about you and Eli."

Her throat tightened. "Yeah?"

"Gossipy old bitch." She heard his booted steps echo across his floor and a screen door squeaked open before slamming closed. "What's new?"

Something in her she hadn't realized she'd been holding on to so tightly relaxed just enough for her to ask the one thing she most wanted to know. "What's the general consensus, Mark?"

"About Eli?" He huffed out a breath. "There are a handful who let old grudges die hard deaths."

"Do they never wonder why he left?" she asked a little more harshly than she intended. "He had to be happy, and no one around here seems to give a damn about that aspect of his life. They're too busy condemning him for leaving."

"Most of them judged him for leaving *you* more than his old man."

Struck dumb, she choked on her beer. When she could finally wheeze without coughing, she asked, "Me? But I left, too."

"And came home." He called out a warning to one of his boys about swinging in the hayloft before returning to the conversation.

"He came home when he was needed. That has to count for something."

"You'd think." Mark sighed and, just as she'd trusted him to do, let the rest of the truth go. "There are a handful of people who believe you're making a huge mistake getting involved with him."

"What you're actually saying is they feel I should continue to live a good widow's life." She blew out a hard breath. "I've reached the point where they can kiss my ass."

"Good girl. Just know the majority of us have your back."

"Thanks, Mark." Winding her ponytail around her hand, she fought the shake in her voice. "That's not why I called, though. Well, not the only reason."

"What can I do for you?"

"You've heard the county's going to be quarantined."

"Yeah," he answered, voice tight.

"It's going to mean lower profits for everyone for a bit. I'm going to cut my service rates to dirt, sell meds at wholesale, do what I can to help. That means I can't keep this place."

"Without the income from the calves, I can't afford to buy it."

"I've got the mortgage paid through the end of the year." Her belly flipped like a pancake tossed by a short-order cook. "If I have an attorney draw up a lease-to-purchase that's favorable for you until you get your calves sold and can make the purchase, are you still interested in buying my place?"

"You sure about this?" he asked gently.

"It's time." Her answer was so quiet the words competed with the crickets emerging for the evening.

"Have your attorney draw it up. You want to stay in the house until we close the deal for good?"

She hadn't thought that far ahead. "It'd be great if you'd be willing to let me. I'll include all my livestock in the sale except the horses. I'll keep those," she said, voice tight.

"You sure you're ready to take this step, sweetheart?" Mark asked, the term of endearment nothing more than one of close friendship.

Even though he couldn't see her, she nodded. "It really is time, Mark."

"Then we've got a deal. And if you need to stay at the house longer, just give me a holler. We'll work something out."

"Thanks, Mark. Good night." Disconnecting, she set the phone down.

Being with Eli had proved to her she'd been holding on to the wrong memories for far too long. When he left this time, she'd mourn him, yes. But she would also be able to celebrate what they'd shared. So from now until he left, she would relish every second they had together. If he could forgive her the quarantine mess.

The rumble of a diesel engine came down her drive and cut off in front of her house. She stood and stretched before starting around the wraparound porch toward the front of the house. The truck came into sight first. It was a Bar C vehicle, and the first thing she thought was that something had gone horribly wrong. Her walk turned into a run as she rounded the corner of the house to see Eli raising a hand to knock. She stopped suddenly, rocking forward. "Eli?"

He looked over at her, face solemn. "I brought a piece of glass to fix the door."

"I already had it done, but thanks."

"Send me the bill, okay? I meant to get to it sooner, but…" He didn't have to explain anything to her. They both knew how hellish the past few days had been.

"Why are you here? What's wrong?"

One corner of his mouth lifted. "Nothing."

"Everything is okay at the ranch?" she demanded.

"As okay as it can be given the fact Dr. Alvarez quarantined the county." He shrugged. "It is what it is."

"I'm so sorry, Eli," she whispered.

He closed the distance between them and wrapped

her in a hard hug that nearly stole her breath. "Don't you dare apologize. You did what you had to do. Yeah, we were pissed about it. Might even have cursed you once or twice, if I'm honest." He drew back and met her stare. "But you didn't cause this. We have no idea where it originated, had no idea initially that it was something so serious. Maybe we could have, even *should have*, moved faster, but Shipping Fever is so rare nowadays. It seemed logical to assume it was something less lethal. All we can do now is get through the aftermath." He swallowed hard and gazed out over her land. Set in the Cimarron Valley, it was idyllic. Nothing as wild and scenic as the Bar C, but pretty enough. "I'm going back to Austin. Soon. I'll have to make some serious financial changes to my lifestyle, but I'm going to do my damnedest to provide the operating overhead Cade and Ty have to have to keep the ranch."

This time it was she who wrapped her arms around him. A slight tremor worked its way through her and down her arms, curling her fingers into his shirt. She didn't want him to leave. They'd barely scratched the surface of what might have been between them. She didn't want to let him go. Not again. Not like this. Not knowing she would, at best, be someone he either visited or simply ran into when he came home to visit his brothers. Breaking away, he grabbed her hand and hauled her toward the truck, but she resisted. "What?"

"I'm barefoot."

Without missing a beat, he scooped her up and carried her to the truck. "Shoes are optional tonight."

"Where are we going?" she asked as he deposited her in the cab.

He crawled in behind the wheel, hooked an arm

around her waist and pulled her close to his side. "Somewhere I should have taken you already."

The most she could do was buckle up and go along for the ride.

14

ELI TURNED ON the radio and sang along with some of the current country hits, ignoring the surprise on Reagan's face that he was familiar with the lyrics. They drove for half an hour without talking, her leaning into his side, his arm around her shoulders. The night was a brilliant blue-black, the wind little more than a breeze. An owl swooped across the highway close enough to make Eli tap the brakes, but the bird was long gone by the time he even reacted.

"Where are we going?" she finally asked.

"Just hang tight."

Highway 64 curved southwest and Eli slowed, pulling off the highway and up to a metal gate. He'd made sure Cade had pulled the key for him so he wouldn't have to dig through the multiple keys on the key ring. Some nights, like now, it paid to appear like you had your shit together.

Gate opened, he drove through, locked it behind him and continued down the dirt road. A glance to the side showed Reagan twisting her hands in her lap, a wide grin splitting her face. "The river."

"Yeah." Her excitement was a huge relief—*huge*—

and he found himself unintentionally speeding up, the washboard road rattling the truck's rearview mirror so wildly it was nauseating. He didn't slow down.

One mile of dirt roads later and two more turns west and he eased off the gas. The rush of the Cimarron River, relatively shallow here but fast moving over rocky areas and hushed in the deeper curve, spilled before them like a wide band of hammered silver in the moonlight.

She shifted to her knees on the seat, grabbed his face and kissed him senseless, all heat and a tangle of tongues. Fisting his hair, she pulled his head back and grinned. "I can't believe you brought me here."

His immediate erection said he should have brought her here that first night. He felt like a kid again, not a thirty-three-year-old lawyer. Smiling in answer, he dragged her across his lap, cradling her in his left arm while he stroked her face with his free hand. "Pretty as you've ever been, but more beautiful in the moonlight than my dreams do justice."

"Careful, Covington," she said, soft and husky. "Words that sweet'll get a guy in my pants."

"Any guy?" he asked, teasing a finger along her collarbone.

"Just one."

He leaned into her, pulling her up so their lips met in a lazy kiss. He nibbled and suckled, whispering to her how beautiful she was, how long he'd dreamed of being here with her, the way the taste of her skin haunted him on sleepless nights—all the things he'd wanted to say to her from the moment he'd first seen her but hadn't been brave enough.

But he understood now there simply weren't any guarantees. Things could be going absolutely right and then the road could end and you'd find yourself in free fall. There wasn't time to waste with her.

Tongues dueling, the taste of the hoppy beer she'd been drinking rolled through his mouth. Their breaths mingled. He nipped her bottom lip, then sucked on it, and when her head tipped back, he traced a line from the hollow of her neck to her chin with the tip of his tongue. Her every gasp, every plea for more—it all drove him crazy. But that wasn't what this night was about. Not in its entirety.

Pulling away, he put a finger over her lips to stop her objection. "We've got all night."

"Yeah?" One corner of her mouth curled up. "Cade lift your curfew?"

"Cade can kiss my ass. I'm out all night." He kissed the tip of her nose. "If you'll have me."

She laughed. "Oh, I intend to have you, all right."

"At least the seduction part of the evening's plans are a go. Takes a lot of pressure off a guy."

"Glad I could help." She scrambled out of his lap and across the seat, pausing when she opened the door. "Don't suppose you've got a pair of irrigation boots tucked between the cab and the bed?"

"Sit tight." He dropped to the ground and went to the rear of the truck, pulling out blankets and a small cooler. "Dig the pillows out from behind the seat."

"Pillows?" she called, the smile in her voice evident.

"Hey, growing up should count for something. In this case, it's pillows."

They flew at him one at a time, and he made them part of the bedroll. Then he went to the passenger side of the truck, reached around her to turn the music up a little, and, before she could object, tossed her over his shoulder. She screamed with laughter, and his heart beat so fast it hurt. So much had changed between them, but not this. *Never again this.*

He carried her to the lowered truck tailgate and set her down gently. "Stars," he whispered, looking up.

She followed his gaze and sighed. "Do you know how many nights, in college in particular, I wondered if you were gazing at the same stars I was? It made me feel closer to you."

"Yeah. Me, too."

He got them settled, her head on his shoulder, a blanket within easy reach to flip over them when the night cooled off. Laying his lips against her temple after fourteen years, he had the most concrete sense of what truly mattered, and it had nothing to do with old hurts or regrets or bad decisions.

They talked for hours, catching up on fourteen years of missing each other. Luke was noticeably absent from the conversation, and Eli was both grateful and curious. Stars filled the New Mexico night sky, so much bigger than he remembered.

What he'd never forgotten was the shape and warmth of the body beside him. He closed his eyes sometime after midnight and let his fingers, his hands, his mouth *remember.* Moving over her, he parted her thighs. She encouraged him closer and he buried his face in her neck.

He breathed her in, the smells of sunshine and warm skin and something soft that was simply her, had always been her. "You're for me, Reagan. You've always been for me. And you always will."

REAGAN'S HEART TRIPPED all over itself. Her hands paused in stroking Eli's back. Hell, she might have stopped breathing. Terror ripped through her. Had he just…

His breath was hot against her skin as he lifted his head and nipped her earlobe. "Living without you has been like living without the sun. I did it, but I don't want to go back to that, don't want to do it again."

She'd wanted this so badly for so long, but she was broken in too many ways. She didn't know what to do. There were too many things to say and not enough words. She didn't want to screw this up, didn't want to—

"I've lived with my mistakes for fourteen years. No more. I won't go another day pretending this is anything other than what it is. It's never been anyone but you. Only you."

She scrambled out from under him, pushing and shoving.

"Reagan?"

Barefoot or not, it didn't matter. She leaped from the truck and took off running for the river. Rocks and grass scraped at her feet. She didn't slow down. Memories chased her too hard and too fast. She was swift enough to outrun them. Almost. But what she had no hope of outrunning was the guilt she'd carried for more than eight years. The knowledge caught her at the same time Eli did.

"Don't," she pleaded, struggling to pull free of his grasp.

"Don't what? Care about you? I can't help it, Reagan. You're the one. You've always *been* the one."

She laughed almost hysterically, gripping her shirt and pulling. Her vision blurred with tears. Everything— her clothes, her underwear, her skin—it all felt too tight.

"If this is about Luke…" Eli swallowed hard and dropped his hand. "Did you love him that much, Reagan?" The question hurt to hear almost as much as it seemed to hurt him to ask.

The emotional floodwaters began to rise at an alarming rate. Reagan shook her head. "Don't. Don't bring Luke into this, Eli."

"If you loved him that much, if what you had with him was more powerful than what we have, not just now but before…" He swallowed so hard she heard it. He moved away stiffly, his words a quiet offering filled with regret and respect. "I'll take you home."

Watching him walk away triggered something in her, something fierce and raw and terrifying. "Stop!" The single, shouted word halted him in his tracks.

"What do you want from me, Reagan?" He angled his head to the side, offering her the dark side of his profile. "You want to rub it in my face that I messed up so bad I can't undo the damage? That I can't—and never could—measure up to the county hero-turned-martyr? Job well done."

Something in his bitter self-reproach resonated with her shame, and she found herself stalking toward him. He faced her just in time for her to plant her hands on his chest and shove. Satisfaction surged through her when he stumbled. "How dare you! How *dare* you! What we had—" The first sob ripped through her. "You left me, Eli! I wasn't enough for you. Wasn't enough to keep you here, to make you happy."

He stood there stunned for a heartbeat before his voice was as raised as hers. "I asked you to come with me! You stayed. You didn't love me enough to take a chance on me! And not once," he hissed, "not *once* did you beg me to stay."

"Don't you get it? I loved you! Love shouldn't ever have to beg." Her eyes filled with unwanted tears. "You should have stayed because you loved me more than you hungered for the idea of escaping. But you didn't. So I let you go."

"And married everybody's favorite son. Clearly you were brokenhearted."

His vitriolic anger forced her back a step. But only because she had to have the extra room to release her own fury. "I was destroyed," she whispered on a broken hiss. "I married Luke because I hoped it might exorcise your ghost. And I failed. *I. Failed.* Luke loved me." She pounded a fist over her heart. "And you know what? I didn't love him in return, not the way he did me. Not even close. And no one ever suspected. No one but Luke," she screamed, beginning to shake. "I didn't love him the way he loved me and he knew. He *died* with the certainty that the only man I ever gave my heart to was *you.*"

Sobs racked her body, the confession torn out of her, the history and truth like scar tissue ripped off a wound that appeared healed but had actually festered below the surface.

Eli closed the distance between them in three strides and wrapped her in his strong arms, ignoring her struggles. "He loved you, baby. I know how that feels, and I'm willing to bet that, if you could ask him, he'd tell you there was nothing in the world he would have changed about his life with you."

"But you haunted me, Eli. Every time I turned around, you were there."

"Did he ever stop loving you?"

She choked on a sob.

"Did he?" Eli demanded.

"No."

Pulling her into him, they faced each other in the moonlight, the river the music to his declaration. "I understand how that feels." He reached for the hem of her T-shirt and lifted. "Let me make up for the past, Reagan."

"Don't leave me again," she pleaded. "Don't walk out on me."

"I don't intend to."

Closing her eyes, she raised her arms over her head and gave herself over to the moment. She needed the physical reassurance of him, needed him to lay claim to a heart he'd long ago abandoned.

It took a moment for her to realize that the turmoil that had kept her emotionally off balance 24/7 was gone. It was just the two of them in that moment.

Luke's ghost was gone.

15

ELI REMINDED HIMSELF to go slow, to truly make love to Reagan, but he was desperate for her, the touch of her bare skin as vital to him as his next breath.

In his desperation, he had trouble unbuttoning her jeans. Through her tears, she laughed, undoing them herself and shimmying out of her pants. The rate he peeled first hers and then his clothes off probably set some kind of world record, but he didn't care. He needed her.

Laying her down on the grass, he slipped into her with slow, measured pressure. She wrapped her legs around his waist and arched off the ground. Grabbing her hips, he went to his knees and lifted, fully seating her on his length and forcing her to support herself on her shoulders. Bending over her, he kissed the valley between her bare breasts. That one taste of her skin wasn't enough, though. He traced each beaded nipple with his tongue, suckling them until she was clawing the grass.

Widening his knees, he began to move. Fighting to keep the tempo slow and sure, he loved her body with everything he had. The night was bright enough to cast their shadows on the grass, and he watched the dark impressions move across the ground.

There was truth in that. They weren't the people they'd been. Maybe they hadn't been ready for each other then; maybe it wouldn't have worked anyway; maybe… who knew. All he was sure of at this very moment was that, as he moved into her slick heat, as she arched higher and tightened around his hard shaft, she was the only woman he'd ever given his heart to. He was hers. And whether she was ready to admit it yet or not, she was his.

Sweat slicked their skin.

She gasped as he shifted a hand to give his thumb access to her clit.

He worked that tiny bundle of nerves, loving her body with every skill he possessed, driving her higher. Increasing his thrusts at the same rate he pressed his thumb against her, he felt her begin to shake. He loved that about her. Loved her uninhibited way of giving him her whole body.

She flung her arms out from her sides and tore handfuls of grass from the ground. "Harder," she pleaded.

He gave her what she asked for, vowing then and there it would always be so. There was nothing she could ask of him he wouldn't give. Wouldn't do. Wouldn't sacrifice. He'd been a fool far too long, and they'd both paid a high price for his pride.

The tremors overtook her and she cried out, her sheath tightening around him until she forced the orgasm out of him before he was ready. But his wants were second to hers. Now. Always. He gave her what she wanted, following her over the edge into the abyss.

The only thing he said was her name, whispering it over and over.

ELI HELD REAGAN until they felt the chill in the air. Scooping his lover up, he gave her a piggyback ride to the truck and set her on the tailgate. Neither of them spoke. There were a thousand things to say, and neither of them seemed sure where to start. Eli was fine with that. He wanted a lifetime with her to get this right.

He had to convince Reagan that coming with him to Austin was not only the best thing for both of them, but it was also the *right* thing. It would have been better if he'd had a chance to plan, to figure out how to approach her. He didn't have the luxury. This night under the stars had been his best shot.

Steeling himself, he settled his hands on her waist. "I have to go back to Austin."

Her fingers stalled against his skin.

Gripping her wrists so she couldn't break free, he shifted until he had positioned himself between her thighs. "Come with me."

Her gaze fell, her hands fisting. "I can't leave the county in the mess they're in. Not now," she whispered brokenly.

"Just come for a long weekend, then. See if you could be happy there." The pleading in his voice was open and obvious, and he didn't care. If he had to get on his knees, he would. "I've got to keep that job in order to make money for the ranch. But I can't just leave you, Reagan. I did it once and I've never been the same. Don't say no. Don't shut me down before we've had a chance to talk it out. Please."

"And after the weekend?"

"We'll figure it out, but this isn't over, Reagan. Not by a long shot."

She took a shuddering breath. Tipping her head back, she stared at the sky long enough he was sure she'd say no. His heart stuttered, his mind went blank. She reached out to trace the line of his jaw, a sheen of emotion evident in her eyes. "A weekend."

"To start."

She nodded, a tear tipping over her bottom lashes. "When do we leave?"

16

Eli returned the little rental car first thing the next morning.

"Eli," the owner said, tipping his hat.

"Sir," he responded, surprised and not at all sure who the man was.

The bell on the door jangled and they both turned as Reagan walked through the door. "Hey, Walt."

Walt Anderson. The name registered with Eli as if he was an amnesia patient regaining bits and pieces of his memories. "I appreciate the car, Mr. Anderson."

"You're old enough to call me Walt at this point, Eli." The man's tone was dry as dust.

"Sometimes I wonder if I'll ever be old enough," Eli muttered.

Walt laughed.

Eli jumped, surprised. He couldn't remember the crotchety old man ever smiling let alone laughing.

Reagan laid a hand on the small of Eli's back. "Any extra charges?"

"Nah. Car's a piece of shit." He grinned mischievously at Eli. "Figured it'd do you a little good."

"I may have a black lung, but that would be her fault,

not yours," Eli said, affecting the same dry tone. "She filled the cab with diesel exhaust."

Walt chuckled. "Hear you're gonna be outta town a bit, Doc."

"About four days," she answered, shifting from foot to foot.

This time it was Eli who reached out with a comforting touch. The old man's eyes were shrewd. "Anything you want to share?"

Reagan laughed. "Nope."

"Not even a hint?" Walt wheedled.

"Wait for the Watsons to call. One of them is sure to come up with something worth discussing." The bitterness in Reagan's voice cut at Eli.

"Bunch of pains in the ass, the lot of 'em. Y'all better git or you'll miss your flight."

Eli's brows shot up. "We made those reservations early this morning."

"It's a small town." Walt tipped his head toward the front door. "Have a safe trip."

Eli HUNCHED OVER to get through the plane door and did a quick head count. He and Reagan were two of three passengers on the flight.

Had anyone tried to convince him a mere week ago that he'd be returning to Austin with the only woman he'd ever loved, he would have laughed. Or punched them in the face. Now? Here she sat at his side, nervously gripping his hand and staring out the window as the ground fell away.

He leaned over and kissed her temple. "It's just four days, baby."

"I feel so guilty leaving when the community is in such a mess."

"Dr. Hollinsworth agreed to cover for you. Also, I had Ty call in a favor. He found out Dr. Alvarez will be in town until at least next Friday. It'll be fine."

She peered over her shoulder, brows creased. "But these people count on me."

"So do I."

Grinning a bit flatly, she shifted to press her forehead against the window and watch the plateau pass beneath them.

They made their connecting flight to Austin without any trouble. He'd booked them seats in business class, and she fussed with him for spending the money. Spoiling her secretly thrilled him. He let her mutter for about three minutes, then he kissed her quiet. The way she melted into his embrace made the extra costs for first class worth every single cent.

By the time they touched down in Austin, she'd relaxed. It had taken Eli pointing out she had a smartphone and could, in fact, be contacted 24/7 if something arose. And he'd reassured her that he could have her home in only a few hours if need be.

His car, an Audi R8, had been a matter of social standing and pride when he'd left. Now he wished he owned a pickup, even an SUV—something she'd be more comfortable in, and, in truth, something a little less glaringly excessive. Instead of lingering on the discomfort, he opened the door for her and watched her carefully seat herself and fish for the seat belt.

Settling himself behind the wheel, he offered her a small smile. "It's just a car."

"It's a car that costs more than most of the houses in Tucumcari," she responded quietly.

His brows pinched together. "Is it a problem?"

"No," she said quickly. Then much quieter, "No."

Ignoring the voice that whispered in his ear that something had shifted, he pulled out of the parking garage and into Austin traffic. Chaos reigned during the lunch hour. She was silent as he maneuvered through the snarl of metallic bedlam and hit the interstate at speed.

He'd just opened his mouth to ask her what was going on when his phone rang.

"Covington," he barked, completely ill at ease.

"From the lack of livestock in the background, I'm going to assume you're in town." It was Stephen Smithy, one of the founding partners.

"Yeah." He pinned the phone between his shoulder and ear as he checked his mirrors, then downshifted and switched lanes quickly, heading for his house.

"Glad you made the right decision." Ice rattled in a glass.

"Scotch with lunch?" Eli asked lightly.

"Drinks and dinner with Macallroy have been moved up to tonight. Man's driving us all mad. It's up to you to salvage this, Eli. We can't afford to lose his business, no matter how much I might like to personally string him up by his... Never mind. Peché. Tonight. Reservations are for seven. Come by the office first."

Eli clenched his jaw. "I've already made plans."

"Do what you have to do," Reagan murmured.

He shot her a hot glance and waggled his eyebrows. "What *we* really should do is take my sauna's virginity. He's been trying to give it up for ages."

Her eyes widened and she mouthed, *You're on the* phone.

"So?"

"Much as I enjoy listening to you talk to your female companion—" Stephen started.

Eli interrupted. "Girlfriend, not companion. She's hot as hell and a doctor, so keep your mind out of my sauna."

"Hold the phone. Eli Covington has a girlfriend?"

"A serious girlfriend," he replied softly. *"Very* serious."

Reagan blushed and tucked a strand of hair behind one ear. The almost shy movement charmed him, and he found himself compelled to take her hand and lace their fingers together.

"Eyes on the road," she murmured.

"It's great you brought a love affair home from the wilds, but it doesn't change the fact you have to be in this office by two this afternoon."

Eli fought to ignore the slight jab about Reagan not being Austin-polished. "I'll be in the office by three, but I've got to be out by four to beat rush hour. That's not negotiable."

"Be in the office by two-thirty. You'll leave when we're done. That's all the compromise you'll get." His boss's tone had shifted just enough to warn Eli that he was pushing the man's tolerance.

"See you then." Eli disconnected before Stephen could decide he wanted Eli in the office immediately. He tossed his cell down, fighting to unclench his jaw. "I'm going to have to go into the office for a little while this afternoon. Shouldn't be more than an hour, hour and a half tops."

She slid her gaze to him, color riding her cheeks and mischief in her eyes. "Gives me time to talk to your sauna about his expectations and reassure him I'll be gentle. He can let you know how it was for him when you get home."

"You…" Eli's mock incredulity was ruined when he

had to adjust his swelling cock. Damn, but the idea of her in his sauna, naked, touching herself…

"Eyes on the road, Covington." Her admonishment was tinged with laughter.

He blinked rapidly. It didn't matter what they discussed this afternoon in the office. Eli's mind would be on Reagan.

REAGAN WATCHED THE immensity of Austin spread out as they headed toward the outskirts of town. The homes grew larger, lots became rolling fields and driveways were gated. Appearances were clearly important here, and the realization left her tugging at her jacket sleeves.

She'd dressed in the closest thing to nice clothes she owned—slacks, a jacket and a pair of heels—but she suddenly felt frumpy. She considered herself a simple woman with an appreciation for nice sheets, spontaneous picnics and nights—particularly passionate ones— spent by the river. Riding in such an expensive car with an obviously highly influential attorney as they passed by expensive neighborhoods left her out of sorts, her emotions frayed. Then Eli pulled up to a gated community called The Canyons. He entered a personal pass code and the iron gates swung open.

"The community is built along the edge of Lake Travis. It's quiet. And the neighbors are really nice."

He sounded as if he was trying to sell her on his address. She peered out the window at huge houses. A woman at her mailbox waved as they drove by. She was dressed in kitten heels, silk slacks and a lovely sleeveless shell, and her makeup was subtle but perfect.

Reagan slid a little lower in her seat. She'd never fit in with people who lived like this, and she didn't want to. No way could she stay here and play dress up to walk to the curb for the mail. She wouldn't pretend to have anything in common with people who would never understand her.

"What's bugging you, Reagan?"

She chanced a quick glance his way, shocked to find him clearly confused. "Seriously? Look at me, Eli. These are the best clothes I own, and I wasn't as well dressed as the woman picking up her *mail*."

He sped up, pushing the boundaries of acceptable speed through the subdivision until he pulled into a large half-circle drive. Shutting the car down, he unbuckled his seat belt and twisted to face her. "Stop it."

She hardly heard him. The house he'd pulled up in front of was enormous, easily five thousand square feet. A combination of stucco and stone, it was stunning. A high entry advertised a tall two-story entryway with a wrought-iron chandelier showcased behind a large window. What appeared to be hand-carved double doors were decorated with more wrought-iron work that matched the railing on the wide steps that led to the deep porch. The landscaping was immaculate. Through the sidelights, she could see through the depth of the house and, in the background, the shimmer of Lake Travis.

"Reagan?"

"You live here? Alone?"

"Yeah." He seemed to struggle with what to say and finally, on a sigh, said, "It was a good investment."

"It's a *huge* investment."

He gripped the steering wheel with one hand, wringing it so tightly the leather creaked. "I put far less into this house than I'll be putting into the ranch. Why does this bother you so badly? It's just a house."

"Uh-huh." She faced him. "And this is just a car. And

the credit card you made the travel arrangements with wasn't black. And your lifestyle is really only representative of what anyone who goes to college should expect, right?" Her heart fluttered in her tightening chest.

The realization he lived like this, that he could truly afford to fund the Bar C's recovery efforts on his own? It made her doctorate seem insignificant and the fact she'd agreed to sell off her place a little harder to swallow. Eli would've been able to sell his house here and probably buy her land in New Mexico. In cash. Then it struck her. "With all this disposable income, why did you balk at the cost of treatment for the Bar C's herd?"

Closing his eyes, he took a deep breath before opening them to meet her gaze. "When I first got there— to the ranch, I mean—I was interested in getting in, doing what needed to be done and getting gone. And to be honest, I didn't even *consider* that my brothers might accept more from me. Things…changed." The tightness around his eyes softened. "My brothers and I realized we respected each other. Beyond the respect? We're brothers, Reagan. Neither time nor my absence changed that. I would have done anything to keep the ranch in their hands. But they're proud. I knew Cade would struggle with his pride before accepting the gesture. I wasn't sure how Ty would react. Ultimately? I managed to handle it so neither had a choice. Still, I would have done it for them even if they'd fought me on it." He lifted one shoulder and glanced away. "Bottom line is that they're my brothers and I love them."

Blinking slowly, she nodded, more to herself than in acknowledgment of his statement. He'd told her he cared about her. He'd said repeatedly he wasn't going to leave her again, wouldn't walk away. But he hadn't said he loved *her*.

"Is there something I can say to make this easier?"

What was he—a mind reader? "No," she answered quickly, forcing herself to smile. "Show me around the house?"

He considered her for a moment, then got out of the car. Walking to her side of the car, he took her hands and hauled her from the low-slung sports coupe. The sun's heat radiated off the pavement, dry and unforgiving.

"Listen to me," he said, voice low and fervent. "This is how I've lived, yes. But it doesn't change who I am. I'm Elijah Covington, the kid from Harding County, New Mexico, who grew up driving beat-up trucks and eating beans from a can after my mom died."

She nodded a little too quickly and gave him the honesty that was burning her up inside. "You can dress it up a hundred different ways, but this lifestyle is as foreign to me as if I'd been dropped into another country." Fine tremors ran down her arms, and he tightened his grip on her hands as if she'd run. And she'd be lying if she said the thought hadn't crossed her mind. "This might have been a mistake."

"Hush," he said, the word thickened with harsh desperation. "Don't reject me because of my address or the kind of car I drive. This is all temporary. I'm selling it all off to fund the ranch. We can make this work, Reagan. We can find a place outside the city with a little land where you could run a large animal practice and I can do some telecommuting. All I'm asking is that you remain open to the possibilities."

The laugh that escaped her was tinged with more than a little mania. "You make it sound so easy."

"It can be." At her skeptical look, he squeezed her hands quickly. "More than. Because we'll be in it together."

Somehow, that didn't afford her the kind of reassurance she wanted, but she didn't argue with him. Instead, she gave a short nod, followed him to the front door and into a house that she knew would never be her home.

17

ELI COULD TELL SOMETHING was off with Reagan. She sought his permission to use the computer. Instead of grabbing a soda from the fridge, she asked if he'd mind if she had one. She was withdrawn, always scanning her environment, forever tugging at her sleeves or touching her hair.

The change in her depressed him. It also made him take a hard look at how he'd been living for the past few years. He'd been successful, yes, but he was living a life of unnecessary excess. No way did he need a house this large or a car that cost more than the median income of the Austin population. The realization left him uncomfortable in his own skin for the first time since he'd left home, and he didn't relish the experience.

Reagan had taken a call earlier, leaving him in his room as he changed to go into the office. When he'd tracked her down in the living room, she'd been hanging up with the state vet. He'd quarantined two more ranches today and was beginning to develop a suspicion on the source of the infection, but he was keeping all information close to his chest.

Eli knew the families who'd be affected by the BRD

quarantines, and he'd offer pro bono legal services to every single one of them until this was cleared. And he might even keep his New Mexico license active after that, just in case. If he'd learned anything over the past couple of weeks it was that life thrived on unpredictability.

He closed the distance between them, regret at having to leave her here making every step heavier than the last. "I've got to head into the office. I should be back before five, though."

She flashed him an irritated glance.

Stepping into her personal space, he encouraged her to meet his gaze. "What's eating at you, Reagan?"

She closed her eyes and shook her head. "Nothing worth discussing."

"Try me," he pressed.

"I don't belong here, and I hate feeling like a fake. I'm capable of looking the part but, no matter how hard I try, I'll never really fit in here." She waved her hand in the general direction of the neighborhood before settling her hands in her lap. Picking at a cuticle, she only stilled when Eli reached out and laid his hand over hers. She glanced up, haunted understanding in her eyes. "This is how you felt, isn't it? Growing up in New Mexico? Like you didn't belong no matter what you did."

He nodded, the observation so astute his throat tightened, making it difficult to breathe.

Reaching out, she gripped his hand. "I never got it. I'm sorry for that."

"How could you have understood?" He pulled free and stepped away, walking to the patio doors and staring out over the infinity pool and to the lake beyond. "You were always so at home there, so comfortable. You belonged from the beginning. It was impossible for you to imagine it could be any different for me as another rancher's kid."

"And now?" she asked quietly.

He shrugged. "It's different."

"How?"

Explaining would take more time than he had. Still, he owed her at least a rudimentary attempt at defining the differences. He returned to her, grasping both her hands. "Let's talk about it when I get back."

Her eyes searched his for several seconds before she nodded. "Okay."

"I want to take you out tonight, show you around the city, visit some of my favorite haunts and then maybe take a walk through the heart of the music scene." He rolled his shoulders. "I want to show you the city that's been my home for fourteen years."

"We could stay in and I could cook for you." Her suggestion was offered with almost no inflection.

"Why wouldn't you want to go out to dinner?"

"I just thought a quiet night at home might be nice." She shifted from foot to foot. "And frankly? I'm not sure I'm up to diving into city life."

Totally disregarding his suit, he pulled her lithe body against his. "It doesn't matter what we do, sweetheart. Whatever it is, we'll spend tonight together."

She started to say something, but he bent his head and kissed her. It was meant to be a swift kiss, but it quickly evolved, becoming a drawn-out, slow burn. Desperation weighted every movement and made it raw in a very brutal, real way. There was an unspoken reminder that this opportunity to rediscover each other was fragile and should be treated with the utmost care.

Eli wished like hell he had even a single clue how to manage that. If only do-overs came with manuals that guaranteed a guy could learn from past mistakes and not repeat them.

Unease settled at the base of his spine and slowly burned its way up. He would hurt Reagan again if he botched this up. She'd given him that power over her, the move subtle but undeniable. Conversely, he'd done the same when he'd handed his heart over to her. He couldn't be sure she realized the exchange had been a fifty-fifty trade on the power grid, but when things were just right, he'd tell her how he felt.

It just wasn't something he could blurt out, though. Offer it up too soon and she'd think he wasn't sincere. Wait too long and she wouldn't believe it was genuine. There was a window, a brief moment, when he could convince her that what he felt for her was real. He could only hope he was smart enough to recognize it.

Reagan pulled away and met his somber eyes with bright ones, her lips swollen and parted slightly as she gasped a bit to catch her breath. "Well," she said, putting some distance between them and straightening the collar of his shirt. "That's one way to get me to go to dinner with you."

He chuckled. "There's another way?"

She grinned. "Go to the office and do what you have to do, Esquire. While you're gone, I'll come up with a list of ways you might be able to convince me that Austin's charms are exactly what this country girl can't live without." She spun away from him and started up the winding staircase, the sway of her hips mesmerizing.

Eli was more grateful for that moment than he had been for nearly anything in his life that had come before. The woman he loved was currently in his home, headed to his bathroom to soap up, then get all polished so he could take her out. Her belongings—travel-sized or not—were on his vanity counter. Truth slammed into him with runaway-train velocity, knocking him completely off the tracks. He never wanted to be without those small reminders of her again. Ever.

But for now, he had work to do. Then he had a woman to please. And if the sway of her body was any indication, she was telling him just what she wanted. He intended to deliver. And after that? After they had a little fun this weekend and Reagan saw what their life together could be like?

He'd find a way to make her stay.

REAGAN WOKE FROM her short nap when her cell phone alarm sounded. She stretched, Eli's luxurious bamboo sheets sliding across her bare skin. The bed was so sumptuous she promised herself she'd be getting the same setup when she went home. The mattress, the sheets, the pillows—it all tempted her to stay in bed the entire weekend. The man who would be home soon was an even greater temptation.

Her connection to him was stronger than ever, and she wondered for what had to be the thousandth time if what he experienced with her was anything remotely close to what she found in his arms. He'd said repeatedly he cared for her, had brought her to Austin to share his life with her, but she was still lacking that one fundamental admission that would change everything.

Granted, it had been fast for love. A week? Not so likely. But they'd loved each other before. Yes, they'd been kids, but neither age nor the passage of years could diminish what they'd had together. At least not for her. Was that it? Had he stopped loving her at some point over the past fourteen years and was now only easing his way back into the relationship? Or would they trek down the same path where love wasn't enough to get them through the rough patches?

The thought made her want to throw up. Distracting herself seemed prudent, so she shoved out of bed and went to the sumptuous bathroom, turned the shower on and stepped under the stream of hot water. She didn't really have the best clothes to wear to a nice restaurant, but she'd manage. Maybe mix up her jacket with jeans and boots, put her hair up and pay a little extra attention to her makeup. Whatever she did, she wanted to be beautiful and sexy for Eli.

A couple of hours later, she assessed the completed look in the mirror. She was satisfied that she'd transformed herself into the kind of chic and urbane woman Eli would be accustomed to and, likely, expect.

And she hated it. This wasn't her. She wasn't the girl who sat around and waited for her moneyman to come home. She'd worked long and hard to build a life on her own terms, to be proud of who she was. Eli had helped her to do that. And she wouldn't move backward. Not even for him. When he came home, she'd make it clear that he'd either have to adjust and take her for who she was or she'd return to New Mexico.

Alone.

18

THE DAY HAD been interminable. Eli's boss had ridden his ass about having his priorities skewed over this thing with the family. Alternately, Eli's family had ridden his ass via texts and cell about not getting in touch to discuss operational budgets and options for moving forward under quarantine. They were in limbo, and Cade and Ty did not *do* limbo.

Eli understood that. But what they all failed to realize was that he had more responsibilities than an emotional pack mule, and whipping his ass raw wasn't going to do anything but make him lock down.

After an hour in the office, though, just about everyone had the picture. Lynette had all but disappeared, opting to work in her office instead of his. She'd muttered something about "toxic proximity" as she left earlier.

Macallroy had called three times after somehow finding out Eli had come in a day early, and had insisted dinner be moved to tonight. No negotiation, no compromise, nothing.

Eli immediately thought of Reagan. He'd promised to take her out, and she was already sensitive about how she fit into his life. But when he suggested bringing a date, Macallroy made it clear he had no intention of tolerating interlopers to what he obviously anticipated would be a six-course ass-kissing.

Eli had no intention of going anywhere near that wrinkled bum. No amount of money was worth it, and maybe Reagan could lighten the mood.

Then Stephen laid it out in no uncertain terms. "Macallroy called." The man hadn't said "again," but the implication was loud and clear. "It'll be the two of you at dinner."

Eli slouched low and swiveled his chair around to face Stephen. "My girlfriend's in town. I can't just leave her at home."

"I don't care if you pay Lynette overtime to take the woman to the circus," Stephen spat. "You're going to dinner alone."

"So I can sit down with Macallroy and listen to his threats, take his abuse and simply nod along while he insults the firm, Stephen?" Eli slowly stood and toed the chair aside, propping a hip on the corner of his desk and crossing his arms over his chest. "An impartial witness is a good idea."

The older man arched a silvered brow. "And you truly believe your woman's impartial? Juries are generally malleable, but even I can't imagine them following your skewed logic."

Eli's jaw clenched as he fought the urge to snap at the man. Seconds from the mantel clock in his office ticked by with the unrelenting precision of marching soldiers. Stephen made the move to leave, and Eli shoved off his desk. "You're not being reasonable. This is her first night in Austin—it's important that I spend it with her, keep her with me and make sure she knows she matters. It's not reasonable to expect her to accept the fact I brought her home and then immediately left her, expecting her to fend for herself with no car, no friends and no knowledge of the area. You're standing there insisting I treat Macallroy like a benevolent king while also demanding that I treat my girlfriend like an inconvenience. That's not even remotely equitable treatment, and you know it. There's no reason Macallroy can't wait until tomorrow night for dinner, as was originally planned."

The founding partner paused in the doorway. "Stop thinking with your cock and get your priorities straight. This dinner is about preserving one of the firm's top three revenue-generating clients. If that means Macallroy wants to yank your chain a little and get you to grovel, you'll do it. I don't give a damn what you do with your girlfriend or what excuse you make for having to bow out of whatever you had planned." Stephen shifted to offer his profile, but Eli didn't miss the cold visage on the man's face. Eli had never wanted to be on the receiving end of that look and, until now, had managed to avoid it. No longer. "You do a single thing to screw this up tonight, and your position as partner here is done."

Eli's stomach tightened as if a giant fist had squeezed his innards and turned them into a pulverized mess. "I started in the mailroom here fourteen years ago. I've been loyal to you and this firm, working nights, weekends and holidays, and all in the name of taking care of clients. I have billable hours no one here can match and have managed to secure some of the firm's top clients. You'd let me go because I'm asking a client to hold to his original *dinner plans*?"

"You said it yourself," Stephen said quietly. "This is

about loyalty and where yours lies, Eli. Nothing more, nothing less." With measured steps, the man left the spacious corner office.

Eli spun away from the doorway and looked out over Austin's premier business district. The streets teamed with life. Vendors hawked their wares at street corners. Entertainers had seated themselves at intervals along the sidewalks to play and accept coin or the occasional dollar bill someone might flip their way. The pedestrians ranged from college students to suburbanites to high-end business people.

The view from his window had always been one that energized and grounded him. He'd survived in this city, *his* city, for fourteen years. Some of those early years had been miserable as he survived on ten-cent noodle packets in order to have enough money to make the rent. He'd worked until he'd earned the respect of his peers and superiors.

The haunting voice of his old man had faded over the years, the taunts that he'd never be anyone had faded from memory with every pay increase, every promotion, every accomplishment Eli claimed as his own.

But in the course of one very short afternoon and an even shorter conversation, Stephen had managed to fracture Eli's surety that this was where he belonged. The man had suggested Eli set his morals and ethics aside and cater to the highest bidder—in this case, Macallroy—if he wanted to experience continued success.

Gathering his things and shoving the case file and his laptop into his briefcase, Eli started for the door. His temper was brewing. No one called his ethics into question or suggested he set them aside in exchange for the almighty dollar. Screw that. He'd manage dinner tonight, but then he had to truly reassess what it meant to stay with the firm. His brothers had remained proud and strong while everything they'd worked for had been systematically destroyed. He would do no less.

His phone rang. A quick glance at the caller ID showed Stephen's extension. Hesitating, Eli rested his fingers on the receiver and then pulled away...empty handed. Stephen had made his position clear. There was nothing left to say. Spinning on his heel, he stalked out of the office, his suit jacket flapping over one arm.

From the curious looks a handful of colleagues shot his way, they'd either overheard Stephen's threat or his boss had advertised it to a select few who would make sure the gossip spread.

More intimidation tactics. He'd watched the old man work long enough to expect this, to know exactly how he'd be treated. Stephen had drawn a line in the sand, and if Eli crossed it, he'd be fired, his reputation ruined and all hope for funding the ranch's recovery destroyed.

He missed the elevator by seconds, so he hit the Down arrow and waited for the next one.

Heels clicked across the lobby's wood floors. "Mr. Covington?"

He lifted his face and stared at the ceiling. "Yes, Lynette?"

"Mr. Smithy tried to catch you in your office before you left," she said, voice breathy.

"Apologies for neglecting Stephen's call," Eli murmured. Then he turned his gaze toward the woman, whose face was flushed and eyes wide. "What did he want, Lynette?"

She wrung her hands together. "He said that, before you left the building, I was to tell you that only a fool would throw his career away over a piece of ass, and he's never considered you a fool."

"You can inform him that his message was delivered. Thank you, Lynette." The elevator chimed its arrival with a soft note before the doors silently opened. Eli stepped inside and faced the front of the elevator, meeting his paralegal's paranoid stare. He leaned one shoulder against the wall, the corners of his mouth kicking up with undisguised insolence. "Go home early tonight. You put in way too many hours."

She grinned. "Yes, sir."

The doors slid together and Eli closed his eyes, reveling in the silence.

If he saved his job to protect the ranch, he'd hurt Reagan. If he ruined his career to protect Reagan, he'd hurt his brothers.

There was no way to win. To lose, though? It seemed there were infinite choices available to him.

He only had to settle on one.

REAGAN HAD JUST finished refreshing her makeup when she heard the front door slam and Eli call her name. "Up here!" she shouted.

He came into the room and smiled at her over her shoulder, the action reflected in the mirror, but the smile never reached his eyes.

She rounded on him slowly, makeup brush clutched in one hand. "What happened?"

Closing the distance between them, he leaned in and laid a tender kiss on her lips. "You look absolutely stunning."

She didn't comment, didn't blink. "Seriously. Is everything okay?"

"Yes." He shook his head and raked his fingers through his hair. "No. I've been ordered to attend dinner tonight with the very client who's been raising hell since before I left for New Mexico."

"The one you broke the window in my door for so you wouldn't miss the conference call?"

"That would be the one." He shrugged out of his suit jacket and tossed it across the counter before leaning against the wall, chin tucked into his chest. "I don't want to have to do this, Reagan, but he's demanding I come alone. He wants me one-on-one to ensure I sufficiently kiss his ass and make empty promises that the firm will do all we can to get the EPA fines and settlement figure lowered." Eli looked up. "Don't suppose I could talk you into a rain check on dinner?"

Drawing a deep breath, she set her brush down and propped both hands on the counter. "You went into work this afternoon at their demand, and now you're going to leave me here, alone, in order to go to dinner with a client, again at their demand."

He sighed. "Pretty much."

Rising to her full height, she faced Eli. "That's not what I came to Austin for, Eli. This, being second to your job day *and* night, isn't what I want, and it's certainly not what I'm worth." The truth hung between them, her words heavy, the uncensored guilt in his eyes telling. "I'm not the person whose life revolves around her partner's availability, settling for the scraps of time he can scrounge up on weekend afternoons or the occasional weeknight he makes it home for dinner. I won't be that woman, Eli. Not even for you."

"Come with me." The invitation, undoubtedly sincere, didn't disguise the panic in his voice.

"If that were an option, you would have invited me first instead of asking for a rain check."

"It's an option if I make it one. And I want you to

be there with me. I want you to be a permanent part of my life, not a space-filler." He stepped closer to her, running his hands from her shoulders to her fingertips. "Please come."

She gestured to her outfit of slacks and a sleeveless shell paired with low pumps. "Is this sufficient dinner attire?"

Eli visibly paled even as one corner of his mouth lifted. "Unfortunately, no. But we can run by an upscale shop and pick up something more appropriate. My treat," he added, as if that would sway her.

"Now you want me to play dress up in order to impress your client," she said.

"The restaurant is very high-end."

That would be a *yes* to her question.

Exactly what she'd decided today she would never do. Pretend to be someone she wasn't. Give up the identity she was proud of.

Her chest ached hard and fast as if someone had reached in and pierced her heart. A tiny pinprick. Nothing more. But it was enough to let her know it was enough she would bleed out. Maybe not tonight, maybe not tomorrow, but eventually it would become an inevitability.

It was over, this thing between them. She had to tell Eli. No doubt he would do his best to persuade her to stay, and the man could be very, very persuasive. But she wouldn't let him take over her life again. She wouldn't spend years waiting on him to figure out she mattered more than whatever Austin held for him. No, she would make plans to return to New Mexico tomorrow. Loving Eli would always be her first instinct, but living in Austin would gradually evolve and that love would become resentment. That was one thing she could never allow. What they had was unique, had survived the trials life had thrown their way. Maybe, someday, their paths would cross and they would be right for each other. But that time wasn't now. Her breath hitched.

Eli pulled her into his embrace. "Talk to me, baby. It doesn't matter what you wear. All I care about is that you're with me."

Had she been wrong? Maybe she'd been too hasty to assume that she couldn't be herself in Austin, couldn't be Eli's partner. She could give him—them—this one opportunity. She'd be here tonight anyway, so she would take the chance, go to dinner and find out where things stood. How he was with her in front of a client would be very revealing.

"You'll smudge my makeup." She wiggled free of his arms and started for the stairs. "If we're going to have time to pick up something appropriate for me to wear, we need to go now."

He didn't answer her, simply went into his closet and began to change into more formal attire.

She would play this game tonight with one goal in mind: figuring out who truly held the strings to Eli's heart.

19

Eli had picked out a black Chanel suit, clutch and sky-high Jimmy Choos for Reagan before cajoling her into having her hair and makeup redone quickly at a tony salon nearby. She was beautiful. The loose chignon emphasized the long column of her neck. Smoky eye shadow made her green eyes luminescent.

But with every change he'd asked for, he'd put a certain amount of distance between them. He wasn't a fool—he knew she was withdrawing. Still, he wouldn't give up, wouldn't lose her. He'd fight to find a way to salvage their relationship he didn't want to give up and the career that the ranch couldn't afford to survive without.

She was quiet on the way to the restaurant, staring out the window as she fidgeted with her handbag, snapping it open then closed repeatedly. When Eli laid his hand over hers, she'd stilled but refrained from comment.

He pulled into the valet lane and put the car in Park, waving the attendant off for a moment. Shifting in his seat, he took a fortifying breath and let it out slowly. "This is going to be a difficult dinner."

"I gathered as much when you buffed and polished your balls before dressing," she said calmly.

His lips twitched. "I did no such thing."

"You also did the same to your ass. You're prepared to bend over the barrel for this guy." Her eyes narrowed. "I've got to say, Esquire, I'm not the least bit impressed with your willingness to give it up to someone else on our first official date, particularly when you had me dressed up like a pretty doll."

"I'm not giving it—" His lips clamped together, nose flaring as he fought to rein in his temper. "This is a delicate situation. You're right about one thing, though. It's literally my ass on the line if I lose this man's business, so yeah, I might be a little..." He ran a hand around the back of his neck and pulled, searching for words.

She reached for the door handle, but Eli grabbed her wrist.

"I'm sorry, Reagan. Truly. After we get through this evening, we'll make this whole thing work out the way it was supposed to."

The small flare of hope in her green eyes made him want to scrap dinner and go straight to planning their future, but there wouldn't be as much to discuss if he lost Macallroy's business.

Squeezing her wrist tightly, he gave the valet a short come-ahead gesture. "You look amazing tonight. Just watch my back so the old man doesn't shiv a kidney when I'm facing the bar."

Shaking her head on a chuffed laugh, she took the valet's hand and rose from the low-slung car.

The front of the restaurant gave off a hip vibe. An eclectic array of well-dressed people waited outside; the warehouse district was already coming alive as the sun set. Eli bypassed the line, slipped through the coat check station and discreetly slipped a bill into the hand of the maître d'. "Table for three. I believe my personal assistant requested the private tasting room."

"You're Mr. Covington." The statement was delivered with smooth assurance. "I was advised there would only be two in your party this evening. Mr. Macallroy has already arrived."

"Of course he has," Eli responded just as smoothly. "I'm sure you'll accommodate my companion, Dr. Matthews, and see her seated with us immediately."

"Absolutely, Mr. Covington. Dr. Matthews?" The middle-aged man swept an arm wide, encouraging Reagan to step behind the near end of the bar and through black swinging doors. The noise from the club abated, and the maître d' said, "Please watch your step, Doctor. The metal grates of the stairs might catch the heel of your shoe if you're not diligent."

"Thank you." She took the stairs on her tiptoes, and all Eli could think was that if it had been him, he'd have one big-ass charley horse by the time he made it to the top of that spiral staircase. Reagan didn't even whimper.

"This is where the club was run in the 1920s when prohibition was in full force. It's why you'll hear nothing from below any more than someone from below will hear you."

Reagan shot him a look over her shoulder. Eli grinned, shook his head and pointed to his kidney. She hid a laugh as they cleared the top of the stairwell.

Moving in close to her, Eli nodded at the liveried man and, placing his hand on Reagan's back, directed her to the only table in the moderately sized room.

Covered in black linens and white china, and with candles burning strategically around the room, the table seemed almost suspended in a void. Eli pulled Reagan's chair out but held her elbow to keep her from sitting down. "Don, this is Dr. Reagan Matthews."

The old man stared up at her with an indifference he could only have achieved if he'd tried. Hard. "Mr. Macallroy." Reagan inclined her head and slipped into her seat. "I understand if it's too difficult for you to rise and greet your guests. Please, don't be inconvenienced."

Both men stared at her, startled. For Eli that was quickly followed by panic and fury. He'd explained to her on the way over what this evening meant, that it was a delicate dance. Now, before the old man had even spoken, she was already provoking him.

Stephen had warned him, had told Eli not to bring her, that it would only make the situation harder to control. But Eli had let Reagan supersede his common sense. And they were all going to pay for it if he didn't rein her in, and quickly.

Pulling up a chair, he missed Reagan's arched brow until he was seated and she'd slid her own chair in. Frustrated, Eli grabbed his glass of water and took a short swallow. "Have you ordered from the bar already, Don?"

The old man offered him a cold stare. "I'm not here for shallow, congenial conversation any more than I'm here to play nice with your newest piece of ass."

Eli's temper flared higher, his lips thinning. A feminine hand squeezed his knee.

"I find that hard to believe," Reagan said quietly, leaning back as she let the waiter settle her napkin in her lap.

"It was clearly stated you were not to be part of the evening," Macallroy barked out. "This isn't a social dinner. It's about your pretty boy here making it clear to me that his loyalties lie where they should. You're nothing but an annoying distraction from business dealings well above your head."

Eli's spine stiffened and he leaned toward Macallroy, but Reagan spoke before he could.

"First, if you weren't here for shallow, congenial, *ass-kissing* conversation, you would have answered either yes or no to Mr. Covington's question. You didn't, so you must not be entirely averse to his gesture." She met Macallroy's hostile stare, her face giving away nothing. "Second, if these business dealings were so far above my head that I'd be nothing but a liability to any conversation, I wouldn't be able to discuss your company's public filings, for example, or the public relations nightmare you are facing because of the oil spill. And while Eli hasn't said one word about Macallroy Oil, I have to believe that's a large reason you insisted on meeting with him in person. Your case goes to Federal Court in less than ten days.

"And finally, if you weren't interested in checking out Eli's 'latest piece of ass,' you wouldn't be paying so much attention to my—" she tugged her jacket "—personal assets." She looked up through thick lashes and met his unabashed stare with an open dare to refute her verbal comeback.

Time stalled, seconds dragging by with echoing booms in the vacuum of space created by Reagan's response. As impressed as he was, her words had pulled the safety net out from under the tightrope Eli was walking tonight.

Macallroy didn't tolerate dissidence of any kind, and here she was, heaping it on layer after layer. Every word could be construed as an insult, every look a taunt of what Eli had and Don couldn't touch.

If Reagan didn't cool it, Eli would be fired before they made it to the main course.

The waiter set a glass of bourbon next to Macallroy's right hand so he only had to shift his fingers to retrieve it. He took a solid swallow, blowing fumes through his nose. "You usually don't go for the particularly bright ones, Covington. She's a different flavor for you." Macallroy blinked slowly and focused on Eli. "And while she might be entertaining in a variety of ways, she's pissing me off. Get her under control before she ruins a perfectly lovely evening."

Reagan looked at Eli, clearly expecting him to say or do…*something*.

"Dr. Matthews is my guest, Don. I'd appreciate it if you'd treat her with at least a rudimentary showing of respect."

Don snorted into his glass.

Eli's fist came down on the table. "Enough."

The old man gazed up at him, a slow smile spreading across his face. "I didn't think you had it in you."

"You'll push me only so far before I'll defend—"

"What's yours," Macallroy finished for him. "It's that very fire that led me to retain you six years ago. I'd begun to believe it had been squashed out by soft living and easy women." He barely spared Reagan any acknowledgment when he said, "Though I doubt there's much easy about this one."

Eli shook his head quickly, trying to suss out what Macallroy was really after. "I was under the impression you were prepared to discontinue the representation agreement between the firm and Macallroy Oil tonight. Was I mistaken?"

"No. I intended to see if you were brave enough to bring your balls to the table. You did, so I'm going to give you a chance to convince me you have the same sense of possessive pride in Macallroy Oil's interests as you do your bed partner's. Still, she has to go. Neither my rules nor my standards change."

Reagan sat up straighter in her seat.

If Eli could secure this account, if he could save this line of income for the firm, it would mean much larger bonuses and a faster recovery for the Bar C. But to make his client happy, he'd have to delve into a few gray areas he wasn't proud of, parts of being a lawyer he didn't want Reagan exposed to. His mind flashed to his first meeting with Cade in the sand hills last week. His middle brother hadn't thought he'd cared about anyone but himself. He had to prove to his brothers what they meant to him. It wouldn't be easy, but he was going to get this done for the ranch, for them and, in the end, to afford him the chance at a life with Reagan.

Digging out his wallet, he handed her several fifties. "If you want to grab a table downstairs, baby, I'll be there within the hour. We'll have dinner then."

Reagan glanced between the proffered money and Eli. "You want me to wait. Downstairs."

"I'll have him back to you with plenty of life left in him," Macallroy chuckled, shaking his empty glass at the waiter. "Then the evening's all yours, darling."

Eli stood and helped Reagan out of her chair, his hand at the base of her spine, hastily ushering her toward the staircase. Her heels issued sharp clips across ancient wood floors. "Give me thirty minutes to salvage this account and I'll be out of here. An hour at the most."

She took his cash, tucked it in her clutch and started down the stairs. He saw her pause as he began to return to his client, so he signaled to Macallroy he'd only be a moment. "Reagan? This is important."

She opened her mouth to say something, then closed it, smiling ruefully.

"What?" he pressed, exasperation sneaking into his voice against his better judgment.

"You're right. It *is* important. I just thought… nothing. I finally get it."

And with that, she took off her shoes and skipped down the dangerous treads with far less caution than she'd used climbing up them.

TURBINE ENGINES SPUN UP to a deafening roar as the plane gathered speed down the runway, forcing Reagan deeper into her seat.

She'd left with only the clothes she'd worn to dinner. She'd intended to retrieve her belongings, but when the cab pulled up to The Canyons' gated entry, Reagan had realized she'd never been given the code. He'd escorted her into his life, but it had become very clear he'd never let her in as a person he respected and loved.

She'd said to Eli that she finally got it. And she did. When he'd left her as a teenager, he'd had to go—staying would have destroyed him. So she'd let him go. And when he'd come back, when he'd insisted she should have begged him to stay, she'd told him the truth. Love should never be reduced to begging.

Tonight she'd left because she wasn't willing to beg him to find a way to fit her into a life she clearly didn't belong in. There was no place for her in Austin because if she couldn't fit organically, she'd never fit at all. But the trip hadn't been a total failure. The missing piece of herself she'd never thought to find had snapped into place. Reagan had finally realized she had to have more respect for herself if she demanded her partner offer her the same. That meant she couldn't go back to allowing Eli to be her sole reason for living. She knew herself better now, knew what she was truly worth, and what he'd handed her in cash hadn't been enough to buy her pride. What it came down to was simple, but it didn't assuage the hurt of his loss.

Eli might have her heart, but her life was her own.

20

STANDING IN THE middle of Peché, Eli listened to the maître d' explain he'd called a cab for Dr. Matthews at her request. She'd left through the front doors, alone, more than two hours ago.

Eli realized right then that terror had a definitive taste. Bitter but light, like a mouthful of horribly charred sesame seeds. The foulness coated the inside of his mouth and made it impossible to expunge the flavor. He couldn't breathe without aspirating the charred bits.

He'd known sending Reagan away had been the wrong choice the moment she'd kicked her shoes off and skipped down the steps. Never had he been so divided about what to do—go after her and save their relationship or go back to the table to salvage the client relationship that would allow him to earn enough to fund the ranch's recovery, thus saving his family. Who should garner his loyalty? At that very moment, how was he supposed to determine who came first? He loved both sides fiercely and had no idea how to decide who to see to first. So he'd remained at the table, his immobility making the decision for him.

His cell phone rang and he fumbled with it in his

haste to answer. "Hello?" he shouted above the din. "Hold on. Don't hang up. I've got to get outside. Just— don't hang up!" Shoving his way through the crowd, he stepped into the ever-active warehouse district. "Reagan?"

"It's Stephen."

Eli's shoulders sagged. "I'm a little busy at the moment, Stephen."

"It can wait. Macallroy called and said you brought your stainless steel balls to the table tonight. All he wanted, apparently, was to know you still had them." Stephen chuckled, the cat-who-ate-the-canary sound grating inside Eli's skull. "He also said you brought your girlfriend but managed to shut her down effectively before kicking her to the curb so the men could get down to the kind of talk women weren't created to understand."

Eli stared at the phone's screen, stunned. Without a word, he disconnected the call, opened the Recorder app on his phone and redialed Stephen. The man answered immediately. "Call dropped," Eli said through numb lips. "I only caught part of that. Could you repeat it for me?"

Stephen launched into a repeat of his earlier words, complete with over-the-top embellishments. He openly laughed at the image of Eli standing Reagan up and walking her from the table to the spiral staircase in dismissal. "Did you really shove a wad of cash at her?" Stephen asked, making no effort to disguise the smile in his voice.

Eli's stomach pitched hard enough he braced one hand on his thigh for support. "I did."

"Wouldn't have thought you had it in you, Covington." Stephen chuckled. "Was she pissed?"

"That would be an understatement."

Stephen hooted with laughter. "Good thing you never bother to fall in love with your bed partners. What color was her hair?"

"Light brown." He blinked. "Why?"

"You just need a different color next weekend. Find a blonde, take her to bed. You'll be over this one in no time."

Rage, far too long suppressed, straightened Eli's spine. The guy nearest him took one look at Eli's face, tapped his buddies on their respective shoulders, and the group moved off to give Eli plenty of room. "Shut up, Stephen. For once in your damn life? Shut. Up."

Glass clinked against a stone countertop with a sharp crack. "What did you just say?"

"For fourteen years I've busted my ass, given up almost all of my life for you, attended every social function and toed company policy, reciting the firm's fustian rhetoric to anyone within hearing distance."

"I get you're a little stressed—"

"Stressed?" Eli said softly. "Screw 'stressed,' Smithy. You put me in a position tonight where I had to choose between love and love—for my girlfriend and my family—and there was no right decision to make. If I did right by her, my brothers lost out. If I did right by them, she lost out. But either way? The firm won. Well, congratulations. Your firm managed to retain the biggest asshole in corporate America, but you lost your best lawyer in the process."

Stephen breathed heavily across the line. "Are you threatening me?"

"No, Stephen." Eli grinned. "Threats usually come with demands. I'm simply quitting."

"You're not so stupid as to quit over a piece of ass."

"Refer to her that way one more time, and I swear to you on my mother's grave that I will haul you out of your office and show you how I was taught to handle problems where I grew up."

"You *are* threatening me," Stephen spat.

"No, I'm not. I'm just telling you how it works where I come from."

"You're done here."

"This is why you needed me so bad, Smithy. You were always two steps behind." Eli spun toward the valet desk and started toward the first vested man he saw. "I already told you. I quit."

REAGAN'S RETURN TO her little place was anticlimactic. She'd shed the trim black suit and hung it up, draping it in a garbage bag to keep dust off the fabric. Then she'd put the expensive heels in a brown grocery bag. Tucked in the top of her closet, no one would ever assume the footwear inside cost more than the stud fee on an above-average quarter horse.

The one thing that remained of Eli's extravagance was the lingerie she still wore. She'd chosen it specifically for the fact that the bra did something to her breasts that made them undeniably lush. And the cut of the high-hipped thong emphasized the length of her legs but also made her torso look longer, even leaner. The underwear made her feel pretty, and she liked that. She'd keep it as a reminder of what they'd shared, the hurt they'd overcome and the choices they'd both made. She'd also never wear it again.

Flopping down on the bed, she missed Brisket. She'd have to go out to the Bar C tomorrow and pick him up. Of course, that meant facing the Covington brothers, who would, without a doubt, want to know why she'd come home early. She draped an arm over her eyes and sighed. Maybe she'd wait and go get her dog on Saturday. An extra day wouldn't hurt anyone—least of all her. And, just once, she deserved to catch a break in that particular department.

Pushing off the bed, she shed her underwear and pulled on her favorite boxers and T-shirt, shut the house up and cut off all the lights.

Making her way to the bedroom, she paused in the living room at the sound of a coyote calling somewhere nearby. She'd have to start keeping her rifle by the front door again if they were going to be coming this close to the house. They worked in packs and the group would take Brisket down if they caught him out alone somewhere, and that just wasn't going to happen. She protected what was hers. The universe could kiss her ass if it believed it had the right to keep taking away everything that meant something to her.

The vehemence of her last thought shocked her. Clearly she had some anger issues to work through.

Glancing out the big picture window in the living room, she looked at a night sky full of stars. "Anger issues. Ya think?" she asked the universe at large. Then she flipped it the bird and went to bed.

She didn't delude herself that things would sort themselves out overnight, but she also wasn't stupid enough to turn down the first night's sleep she'd had in years—*years*—where she was the only one in her bed. No husband. No ghost. No memories. No dog. No one but her.

Rolling over, she punched the pillow and fought against the way her throat tightened.

REAGAN SPENT THE next three weeks working her ass off at every ranch but the Bar C. One of the Bar C's cowboys had dropped Brisket off on a run to town, and she and the dog had been making the rounds, pressing forward aggressively in treating every case of Bovine Respiratory Disease that had been reported. She'd crossed paths with the state vet, Dr. Alvarez, as well as the other large animal vet in the area, Dr. Hollinsworth. Both had been spread pretty thin trying to treat the sick herds while isolating the source of the virus.

On the first day of her fourth week home she found herself back at the Jensen place. Some of the calves they'd treated on her last visit had recovered and been cleared to move to stalk fields; meanwhile the ranch continued to treat the few that weren't recovering well. She'd come out today to decide which could possibly be saved versus those for which euthanization would be most humane.

Reagan was on foot, using Brisket to push the yearlings forward into the loading chute, when she had a moment of inexplicable clarity. When she'd been here a couple of weeks ago, she'd been riding the pipe, inoculating animals as they went through the chute to load on the truck. A steer had turned back and pushed his way off the truck. She'd called Brisket in. The truck driver had been helpful in getting things moving again. She'd issued his hauling papers and moved on, thinking nothing of it. Days later, the first animal on the Jensen place had begun exhibiting symptoms.

"Oh, shit." She glanced at that same truck driver as he climbed around the semi's trailer, kicking dried and not-so-dried cow feces off ventilation ports so he could get the gates to latch. This particular trucking company was popular among local ranchers because it was locally owned. Most everyone used them. "Oh, *shit*," she hissed, regret almost choking her.

The drivers were supposed to spray their trucks down with an antiviral if they were working different ranches with the same trailers. But just looking at the condition of this trailer made it clear the trucking company was cutting corners.

The virus was spreading by *truck*. Every time they loaded healthy yearlings into a trailer where infected calves and yearlings had been, they were exposing the healthy calves to the disease. No wonder they hadn't been able to contain it! Every step they took forward had involved moving calves around via truck, thus perpetuating the infection.

The Bar C hadn't been responsible.

Standing on the top rung of the pipe fence, she let out a sharp whistle. Dr. Armando Alvarez and several of the men glanced up. She jerked her chin at Armando before scrambling down. A soft chirp had Brisket at her side. Then she waited, watching the truck driver.

The moment Dr. Alvarez was within earshot, she laid out her suspicions. The look of surprise on his face told her he hadn't considered it, hadn't thought the trucking company might not be following health regulations to the letter.

Armando shook his head, considering the truck driver. "Well done, Reagan. Once it's confirmed, we'll be able to finish treating the remaining sick cattle and lift the quarantine on Harding and Quay counties much faster. I'll call in the FDA and state DoT and we'll get them to take over, since this is their jurisdiction."

"They'll only claim it was their responsibility after we take the fecal samples," Reagan said. "You know they're not going to get their lily-whites dirty when they've got us out here hip deep already."

"Someone's got to be willing to play in the crap," Armando responded, his tone dry as dust. "And in timing that couldn't be more ironic, your lawyer and his posse just showed up."

Reagan forced herself to hold it together. Lifting one shoulder in an elegant shrug, she pasted every ounce of indifference she could summon all over her body. "The lawyer doesn't belong to me."

Armando smiled. "Given the look on his face, I believe he begs to differ. I'm just going to make a few calls from my truck while you deal with him."

"Coward," she whispered at his retreating form. Yanking her hat off her head, she squared her shoulders and rounded on the Covington brothers, her mouth already moving to save them any awkward silences. "We believe the source of the virus has been identified. The Bar C will be released from quarantine in the next thirty to sixty days, provided the disease plays out." Slapping her hat against her thigh, she forced herself to look at Eli. "Congratulations. Appears you won't have to entirely abandon your lifestyle in order to bail the ranch out of debt."

She spun on her heel and started across the corrals. If she could get to her truck, she'd be able to escape. Without distance, she was afraid of what she might say or do, the options running the gamut from emotionally embarrassing herself to finding herself charged with manslaughter brought on by temporary insanity.

"Reagan," Eli called out. "Stop."

She kept walking and would have kept right *on* walking, if he hadn't said just loud enough for her and everyone around them to hear his plea. "Don't make me beg."

21

ELI HELD HIS BREATH. He wasn't a fool. The odds of Reagan giving him a chance to fix this were slim to none. Hell, even if she gave him the chance, it didn't mean she'd let her heart rule her mind. It only meant she'd hear what he had to say before she left him standing in a cloud of dust.

When he'd arrived at the ranch yesterday at noon, Eli had been surprised at the quiet but respectful welcome he'd received from the cowboys in the pens. They'd directed him to his brothers, who'd been up at the house putting together lunch.

Cade and Ty had been happy to see him but wary, both well aware Reagan had returned within a day of leaving with him. It had taken some explaining, a copy of his bank statements and a few raised voices before they'd settled around the table to talk things out.

Eli explained he'd pulled all his available cash together and, in a move of absolute irony, hired an attorney to liquidate his estate and all assets. Eli could've done it himself, but he hadn't wanted to lose whatever hope remained with Reagan. The sooner he could get to her, the sooner he could start to make this right.

He'd made arrangements to pay off the revolving debt he held, from student loans to the balance on his credit card. The cash he held in hand plus what he expected from the sale of his physical property would fund the changes he intended to propose here at the ranch. At what would now be his permanent home. In the midst of all the work he'd been doing to come back for good, he'd come up with a very viable plan to save the Bar C—he wanted to turn the place into a fully operational dude ranch.

His father was gone. He had nothing left to prove to the old man. Eli was proud of the man he'd become, and he had a lot to offer a new business opportunity. He'd only had to convince his brothers.

At first, Eli believed Cade was going to pass out. He ranted and raved about tourists and initial investments and the liability of having kids around the place. But when Eli opened his laptop and shared the potential income figures for the first fully operational year? Cade had gone silent.

Ty had watched and listened, and then he'd nearly driven Eli to his knees. "If it means you're home to stay? I'm in."

They'd talked for hours, his brothers rallying around his idea with more enthusiasm than he could have hoped for. He was stunned by their support of his choice to call the ranch home once again. But it was more than that.

Eli realized for the first time in his life that these two men, his brothers, cared about his happiness. His well-being mattered to them, and their instinct was to put his needs before their own if it meant he got his shot at being happy. It had humbled him, rendering him speechless. It was Ty who'd first understood his dilemma and simply hugged him, thumping him on the back hard enough to knock loose the wedge of emotions between his shoulder blades.

Cade had stepped up to him and held out his hand, his gaze sliding temporarily to Ty and then back. "I'm not hugging you, but welcome home, man. It's been too long coming."

Eli had retrieved his bags, carrying only two suitcases of worldly goods that he'd deemed necessary from his old life. The rest was inconsequential, material stuff he had no emotional ties to. He dumped the bags in his childhood room and returned to the kitchen to find Cade twisting tops off Coors Light bottles and handing them around.

His middle brother took a long swallow and focused on Eli. "How'd you screw things up with Reagan?"

He felt the urge to lie, but he found himself spilling his guts like a teenage girl to her two BFFs. It was miserable. It was embarrassing. It was irritating. But above all? It was painful.

They'd argued about the best way to approach her, but in the end, Eli had put his foot down. "This isn't about you guys. It's about her. And me. And how bad I screwed up. I have to prove to her I'm not the man who shoved her out the door Thursday night and that I want her for who she is. If I can't do that—I don't deserve her."

They'd agreed and a plan had come together, a plan that would make it very clear to Reagan exactly who had possession of his heart.

ELI HADN'T SLEPT a single minute all night. Cade and Ty had hunted Reagan down this morning as planned and, brothers being brothers, had piled into Cade's truck with him and headed to the Jensen place for the emotional showdown.

Now he took a measured step toward her. "I'd like to talk to you," he said softly.

"Stop treating me like an animal that might spook," she snapped.

"Honey, I've never seen so much of the whites of your eyes," Ty called out.

"Shut up, Ty," Reagan and Eli said at the same time.

She looked at him with wary confusion. "What are you doing here?"

Eli shifted his weight from foot to foot. "I came home."

She coiled her hair on her head and pushed her hat on tight. "Well, enjoy your stay." She turned away from him and started for her truck.

"I'm here for good, Reagan."

She stumbled to a stop and wheezed out a single word. "What?"

"I quit my job. A legal firm is liquidating my Austin estate. I'm home. For good. Might practice a little law on the side here if we need the money, but that's another discussion. For now? You need to know I'm here to stay." He stepped forward. "But none of it means anything without you. First, though, I have to apologize. Hear me out. Please."

"You want to apologize?" she nearly shouted as she spun to face him. "Fine. Act like a normal man and pick up the phone. Don't orchestrate an ambush." She issued a sharp whistle and Brisket came to her side.

He'd rehearsed what he'd say to her. He'd planned his approach, practiced his lines, his tone, his delivery. But it hit him right then that this wasn't court. This was life, and he had one shot to plead his case.

"Reagan, stop," he snapped. "You can't run away from this. We *are* going to settle things between us."

"Oh, hell," he heard Cade mutter.

"It gets ugly, you get to pin her, Cade. I'd rather deal with him," Ty said just loud enough to be heard.

She slowly rounded on him, her surprise clear. "You want to do this here? Now? There are witnesses, Eli. The whole world will know everything you say and do. No way to hide it. Not in this county."

"I'll get the Watsons on speakerphone if it'll get you to give me five minutes."

"You keep the Watsons away from me," she bit out.

"Then who? Who do you want to hear this? Name them, and I'll make it happen."

"Why are you doing this?" she asked quietly. "Twice wasn't enough? You need a trifecta of hurts to make sure I'm clear on where you stand?" He saw a hard shiver raced through her before she whipped away from him.

"I want to stand beside you, as your lover, your partner, your husband. For the rest of our lives."

REAGAN TRIPPED TO a stop. "Don't," she said, voice breaking.

"Look at me, Reagan."

She shook her head.

His shadow covered her first, then he moved around her. "You won't come to me, then I'll come to you. From now on, baby. Every time you leave, I'll come to you."

Reagan's heart stumbled in her chest as he took her hands in his. "I can't marry you," she said, voice breaking.

"That's only because I haven't officially asked yet." Pulling a ring from his pocket, Eli went down on both knees in front of her. "You told me love shouldn't have to beg. You were right. But it should be willing to. If begging's the only card a man's got up his sleeve, then it's the hand he plays and pride be damned. I'm not down on one knee, Reagan. You've taken me down to both. This is what I've got to offer you—a lifetime of humility, humor, honesty and…" He scratched his chin then grinned up at her. "Oh, yeah. That other thing. I love you, Reagan Matthews. The strong, proud woman in front of me in jeans, a hat and cowboy boots. I wasn't brave enough to say it before. I kept thinking I'd get around to it when the time was right. And then I almost missed my window altogether. Give me the honor and the privilege of loving you to the end of my days."

In all her years, she'd never expected to find Elijah Covington kneeling in cow crap with a whopper of a diamond ring in one hand, his hat in his other and his heart in his eyes. For her. Only her.

"And if I say no?" she asked quietly.

He swallowed hard. "That's your right. But it's my right to keep asking until you change your mind."

"You ought to know he's got a degree in arguing," Ty called out.

"Shut up," Cade whispered, wiping at his eyes.

"Bro, are you *crying*?" Ty asked loudly. "You're not the one he's asking to marry him."

Cade boxed Ty's ear. "Shut up before your face finds out how deep the sludge is in the stock tanks."

"Shutting up, you big weenie," Ty muttered.

Eli looked up at Reagan. "Don't make me chase you, Doc. I learned the hard way that with the horses these days, a man only gets three swings. This is my third."

"I never stopped loving you," she whispered.

Eli surged to his feet and wrapped her in a hard embrace. "Ditto that, baby. You were always the one. I've never loved another." He leaned away just enough to see her face. "I don't expect to replace Luke. I don't," he insisted when she opened her mouth to speak. "I'd rather honor his memory by taking the best care of you I know how."

"And how are you going to do that?" she asked, smiling up at him.

He kissed the tip of her nose. "By adding your name to the deed to the dude ranch."

"Dude ranch?" she asked, stunned.

"The Bar C will be undergoing major renovations and should be open for business come late spring. We'll be a fully operational dude ranch catering to people who want the true Wild West experience."

"You're insane."

"Based on his numbers, we're going to be making *bank*," Ty called out.

Eli grinned. "I'll have the means to support myself—it will support both of us, actually, if you want to work alongside me. Regardless, you say yes and you'll never be completely free of me again, Doc. Think long and hard on this."

But she didn't need to. "Ty?" she called out, gripping Eli's hand and backing toward the Jensens' barn. "Keep the Jensens out of their barn for a half hour."

She squealed when Eli hoisted her over his shoulder and started for the truck. "To hell with that. We've got a barn of our own. Stay the hell out of it this afternoon, brothers."

"I love you, Elijah Covington," she said softly as he settled her into the passenger seat of her truck.

"And I love you…" he said, and grinned, "Doc Covington."

* * * * *

"I can do almost anything with clay. Pottery is my passion, but I really enjoy sculpting, too. Hang on." Lark smiled and held up one finger, as if Shane would leave the minute she turned around.

She swept into the storage room and bent low to get something from the bottom shelf. And Shane knew it'd take an explosion to get him to move.

Because that was one sweet view.

He watched the way the fabric of her dress sort of floated over what looked to be a Grade A ass, then had to shove his hands into his pockets to hide his reaction.

As Lark came back with something in her hand, she gave him a smile that carried a hint of embarrassment, but unless she could read his mind, he didn't know what she had to be embarrassed about.

"You might like this," she said quietly, wetting her lips before holding out her hand, palm up.

On it was a small, whimsical dragon. Wings unfurled, it looked as if it was smiling.

"You made this?" Awed at the way the colors bled from red to gold to purple, he rubbed one finger over the tiny, detailed scales of the dragon's back. "It's great."

"He's a guardian dragon," Lark said, touching her finger to the cool ceramic, close enough that all he'd have to do was shift his hand to touch her. "You might like one of your own. I can tell Sara worries about you."

Shane grimaced at the idea of his baby sister telling people—especially sexy female people with eyes like midnight—that he needed protecting. Better to change the subject than comment on that.

"It takes a lot of talent to make something this intricate," he said, waiting until her gaze met his to slide his hand over hers. He felt her fingers tremble even as he saw that spark heat. Her lips looked so soft as she puffed out a soft breath before tugging that full bottom cushion between her teeth. He wanted to do that for her, just nibble there for a little while.

"I'm good with my hands," she finally said, her words so low they were almost a whisper.

How good? he wanted to ask, just before he dared her to prove it.

Don't miss
A SEAL'S TEMPTATION by Tawny Weber.
Available in September 2015 wherever
Harlequin® Blaze® books and ebooks are sold.

www.Harlequin.com

HBEXP0815

Love the Harlequin book you just read?

Your opinion matters.

Review this book on your favorite book site, review site, blog or your own social media properties and share your opinion with other readers!

Be sure to connect with us at:
Harlequin.com/Newsletters
Facebook.com/HarlequinBooks
Twitter.com/HarlequinBooks

HARLEQUIN®

A *Romance* FOR EVERY MOOD™

JUST CAN'T GET ENOUGH?

Join our social communities
and talk to us online.

You will have access to the latest
news on upcoming titles and special
promotions, but most importantly,
you can talk to other fans about your
favorite Harlequin reads.

Harlequin.com/Community

 Facebook.com/HarlequinBooks

 Twitter.com/HarlequinBooks

Pinterest.com/HarlequinBooks

THE WORLD IS BETTER WITH

Romance

Harlequin has everything from contemporary, passionate and heartwarming to suspenseful and inspirational stories.

Whatever your mood, we have a romance just for you!

Connect with us to find your next great read, special offers and more.

 /HarlequinBooks

@HarlequinBooks

www.HarlequinBlog.com

www.Harlequin.com/Newsletters

HARLEQUIN®

A *Romance* FOR EVERY MOOD™

www.Harlequin.com